Tom
Time T

by

David Webb

Illustrated by
Jess Richards

First published
September 04 in Great Britain by

Educational Printing Services Limited
Albion Mill, Water Street, Great Harwood, Blackburn BB6 7QR
Telephone: (01254) 882080   Fax: (01254) 882010
E-mail: enquiries@eprint.co.uk   Website: www.eprint.co.uk

ISBN 1-904374-94-8

Chapters

Chapter 1

The Dreamer

Thomas Travis shot bolt upright in bed and stared with wide, frightened eyes into the pitch darkness. His lips were quivering and his hands were shaking; his pyjamas were damp with the cold sweat that caused him to shiver violently from head to toe. It was the same dream. The one that recurred regularly and disturbed his sleep, so that he was gradually becoming more and more tired and grumpy.

Tom had first experienced the dream on the twenty-eighth of February, the night before his eleventh birthday. He was a leap year baby, having been born on the twenty-ninth of February. Of course, he could only celebrate that once every four years so he always told everyone that his birthday was on the first of March. There was no way Tom was only going to have a birthday once every four years. Think of all those presents he'd miss!

It began with a falling sensation. Tom seemed to lurch forward into a never ending black tunnel, tumbling and spinning downwards, unable to release the scream that was trapped inside him. Different scenes flashed past, too quickly for him to register in his terrified mind. There were rivers and hills and buildings; there were faces looming out of the darkness, laughing and sneering as he tumbled ever downwards. The dream always ended the same way. Tom would suddenly jerk upright and he would watch in disbelief as the transparent, white figure of a young girl glided silently towards his bed before fading from view and then disappearing completely.

That first time, he had shouted out in fright and his mother had rushed into his bedroom and snapped the light on. She had wrapped a comforting arm around his shoulders and listened sympathetically as Tom blurted out his dream between sobs and sniffles.

'It's all right, Tom,' mum had said, reassuringly. 'Lots of children have nasty dreams. You're probably a little bit over-excited about your birthday. You'll soon get back to sleep.'

Tom had accepted the explanation but a few days later the dream had recurred, the falling sensation even more realistic, the white figure even more clearly defined before the frail apparition faded from view. Now it had happened again, so that Tom shivered in the darkness and took deep breaths in an effort to remain calm.

The strange thing was that this first dream was often followed by a second dream. Tom slipped back into sleep almost expecting further visions to float into view. Sure enough, images began to form, confused at first and then clearing so that the dream was like a play being acted out in front of him.

Tom was in the play but he was younger,

probably no more than four years old. His mother and father were there, too, and his sister, Serena - his horrible sister who annoyed him so much in real life now that she was thirteen. In his dream, she was still a little girl and she skipped along holding on to her father's hand. They were in a forest and it was springtime. There were bluebells and there were primroses and the leaves, in their newness, were fresh spring green. They had just finished a picnic and young Thomas was watching as his mother shook the cloth free of crumbs before folding it carefully and placing it back in the basket. It was then that he saw the ring drop. His mother's golden ring that had been passed down for generations must have snagged on the cloth. It flew up into the air, glinting in the sunlight that filtered through the forest trees, twisting and spinning before falling to the soft forest floor and nestling amongst the sweet pine needles. His mother hadn't felt a thing and she was completely unaware that her precious ring was missing.

It felt now, in his dream, as if Tom was standing at the edge of the forest clearing watching himself as a four year old move forward to pick up the ring and hand it back to his mother. However, as he watched, Serena broke free from her father and skipped across to Tom. She grabbed hold of her brother's arm and the two of them ran off along the forest path, leaving the golden ring embedded on the forest floor, soon to become a lost treasure.

The clearing was empty but Tom did not feel alone. No birds sang in the trees; no animals rustled in the undergrowth. And then the strangest thing happened. Tom could feel himself moving forward. He stepped from his watching place in the trees and he walked slowly across the forest clearing. He stopped near to where the cloth had been lain with the picnic and he stooped down to forage amongst the pine needles. Tom found the ring within seconds. He held it up so that it gleamed in a shaft of sunlight and then he closed his fist tightly around the tiny golden object and looked up towards the tall trees that towered above him.

It was as Tom turned to walk back into the forest that he saw the three figures. At first, it was just a feeling that someone was watching him. He took a few steps forward and then stopped, the ring clutched tightly in his hand. He stood very still and he listened but there was no sound in the silent forest. It was eerie. Why were there no birds in the trees or small animals scurrying in the undergrowth? Tom scanned the line of trees that surrounded the clearing and, in his dream, he felt his heart jump as he saw the first figure. It was a boy, about the same age as Tom. He had stepped from the cover of the trees and he was standing as still as a statue, staring in Tom's direction. He had brown hair that flopped forward over his forehead and parted like a pair of curtains. He wore

simple clothes, a plain jumper and a pair of denim jeans.

Tom's heart was thumping. He took a few paces forward and then he stopped again, as two more figures emerged from the trees and joined their friend. There was another boy, slightly smaller this time, with darker hair and a sullen face and there was a girl who was also about the same age as Tom. Tom stared at the girl. She was so pretty and she had the fairest hair he had ever seen. It shone like the golden ring that he still gripped tightly in his fist. All three children were dressed the same - a simple jumper and denim jeans.

The first boy took a step forward. 'We've been watching you,' he said. His voice was steady and calm. 'We saw you all those years ago with your family and now you've found the ring.'

'I ... I ... don't understand,' stammered Tom. 'Who are you? What are you doing here? What am I doing here, come to that!'

'We're friends,' said the girl, stepping forward to join the first boy. 'We're here to help you.'

'I didn't know I needed help,' replied Tom, more confidently. 'I'm only dreaming, you know. Lots of children have nasty dreams - my mum says so.'

'So you think it's a nasty dream, do you?' The first boy was speaking again and he moved forward so that he was standing no more than a few metres away from Tom.

Tom considered the question. 'No, not really,' he replied. 'It's quite a nice dream, I suppose.'

There was a fallen tree trunk near to where the boy was standing and he sat down on it, his eyes still firmly fixed on Tom. 'The point is,' he began, slowly, 'you're not really dreaming at all, Tom. You're here, aren't you? You're in the forest with us and you've got the ring in your hand. We knew you'd come. We've been waiting for you.'

The sullen boy moved forward and stood behind the fallen tree trunk. He still had not spoken.

'Of course I'm dreaming!' snapped Tom. 'The ring is just a part of my dream, the same as you are. When I wake up you'll all be gone. Anyway, how do you know my name?'

'We really need to talk to you but we're running out of time.'

It was the fair-haired girl speaking and Tom paid full attention.

'You must come back tomorrow night, Tom. Seek us out in your dreams. We'll be here waiting for you.'

The boy raised himself from the fallen tree trunk and the three mysterious children turned their backs on Tom and walked away towards the edge of the clearing.

'Wait!' shouted Tom. 'Wait! There are things

I need to ask you!'

He started forward but, as soon as he tried to move his feet, he felt himself begin to fall. Tom reached out a hand to cushion the impact of the forest floor but there was nothing there, only darkness. He was spinning and turning again, ever downwards towards the sudden shock of consciousness.

'Tom! Tom! Will you get a move on! It's ten minutes past eight! You're going to be late for school if you don't hurry up!'

Tom's mum shook him again, pulled his quilt down and then drew the curtains, allowing the morning sunlight to flood into his bedroom.

Tom moaned and yawned and turned over so that he was facing away from the window. Tom hated mornings and, since the dreams had begun, he had found it even more difficult to get himself up for school. He lay there for a few more minutes and then he opened one eye very slowly so that he could see his bedside clock, the black figures magnified by the half empty glass of water that stood in front of it. Eight-fifteen. He really would have to make a move, especially if he was to beat Serena to the bathroom. Tom stretched his arms and legs and then opened both eyes wide in sudden realisation. His right hand was still clenched, as it had been when he held it up to the forest trees in his dream. Tom sat up in bed and stared at his closed fist. His fingers were stiff and he uncoiled them slowly, somehow sensing in advance what he would see. He stared in disbelief at the gold ring that nestled into his palm. He transferred it to his other hand, as if to check that it really did exist. He held it up in his fingers so that it glinted in the early morning light, just as it had done when he had retrieved it from the forest floor.

'Are you out of that bed yet?'

Mum's voice shook him into action.

'Yes!' lied Tom. 'I'm just pulling my socks on!'

Five minutes later, Tom was seated at the kitchen table, washed, dressed and ready for breakfast. The ring was in his trouser pocket. He had beaten Serena to the bathroom, much to her annoyance and she was already half way through a bowl of dry looking muesli.

'I don't know how you eat that stuff,' said Tom, filling his own bowl with Cornflakes. 'It looks as if it should be on the bottom of a rabbit's cage.'

'I eat it because it's healthy,' snapped Serena. 'Anyway, it's none of your business what I have for my breakfast.'

Tom stuck his top teeth over his lip and pretended to be a rabbit, which caused Serena to scowl and pull her tongue out at him.

'Don't pull tongues at your brother,' said mum, putting down a pot of tea on a placemat in the centre of the table. 'It's not a nice thing to do.'

'Well, he's weird,' retorted Serena. 'All my friends think he's weird, you know. Why do I have to have a brother who's so weird? Anyway, he's not my real brother, is he?'

Tom knew he was adopted. He had been told several times how he had been found by an old tramp when he was just hours old. It was the twenty-ninth of February, it was cold and it was drizzly and he had been left, wrapped in a blanket, in a cardboard box outside the gates of The Royal Observatory at Greenwich. He had been rushed to hospital where he was placed in an incubator and it had been touch and go for a few days as to whether he would survive. The adoption had taken months, of course, and when Mr and Mrs Travis heard that the old tramp was called Tom, they decided to call their new pride and joy Thomas Travis in his honour.

'You're adopted, too, you know,' retorted Tom. 'You needn't think you're something special.'

'Yes, but at least I'm not weird,' said Serena, and she crammed another spoonful of muesli into her mouth.

'And don't call your brother weird,' continued mum, as she picked up the milk jug and poured a drop into the bottom of two mugs. 'He's just a bit different, that's all. It wouldn't do for us all to be the same, you know.'

'Look at him,' persisted Serena. 'He even looks weird! He's got green eyes and his hair hangs down over his forehead like a pair of curtains!'

'Mum,' began Tom, completely ignoring his

sister's comments, 'I've got a surprise for you.' He reached into his pocket and pulled out the gold ring. He placed it on the palm of his hand and held it out towards his mother.

Serena stared in bewilderment, a spoonful of muesli suspended in mid air.

'What is it?' mum began, and then she jumped back in sudden recognition. The blood seemed to drain from her face and she placed one hand on the table to steady herself. 'Oh, my goodness ...' she panted. 'It's your grandma's ring! The one I lost years ago!' She sat down on the nearest available chair and held out a shaking hand to receive the ring from Tom.

'You dropped it in the forest,' explained Tom, 'when we were tidying up after a picnic. It caught in the cloth and went spinning to the forest floor.'

'But ... but ... I don't understand? That was years ago when you were both small children. Where has it been all this time, Tom? How come you've got it?'

'I told you he was weird,' interrupted Serena. 'And he's getting weirder by the day! He must have kept that ring hidden in his bedroom for the last six years. You can't tell me that's not weird!' And she shovelled the last spoonful of muesli into her mouth before rising from the table and leaving the kitchen in triumph.

Chapter 2

The History Lesson

Tom Travis followed the same routine every morning. He would get up (usually late), argue with his sister over breakfast and then dash out of the house with his jacket half on and his school bag trailing over his shoulder.

Mondays were the worst. Tom hated Mondays. He couldn't see why Monday had to be the first day of the school week. This particular Monday morning was grey, damp and drizzly, which matched Tom's mood perfectly. It was ten minutes to nine and his friends would be waiting for him at the corner of the street. He quickened his pace as he passed Melissa Morgan's house. Dreadful girl. Blonde curls, big eyes and a tap dancing fanatic. He didn't want to have to walk to school with Melissa Morgan – that would put him in an even worse mood.

Tom got to the top of the road and, sure enough, Christopher Edwards and Beefy were there waiting for him.

'Come on!' shouted Chris, as Tom approached. 'You're going to make us late for school again.'

'Sorry,' said Tom. 'I had a bad night's sleep. I got up a bit late.'

'You're always having a bad night's sleep,'

said Chris. 'What's up with you? You're like an old man!'

'It's just that I dream a lot,' explained Tom, as they made their way towards Hollow Lane School. 'Strange, realistic dreams that leave me feeling more tired than before I went to sleep. It's almost as if I've taken part in the dream. I meet people and I talk to them and … well, it's hard to explain.'

'I dream a lot,' said Beefy, enthusiastically. He was a huge lump of a boy. Although he was in the same class as Chris and Tom he looked at least three years older. 'I dreamt I was at a party last night and there was loads of food. You could help yourself to whatever you wanted. There were plates of sandwiches, pies and pizzas; there were bowls of crisps and nuts – and you should have seen the cakes and puddings! I'll tell you about the puddings …'

'No, it's all right, Beefy,' interrupted Chris. 'I think we've got the idea!'

The boys said good morning to Mrs Briggs, the lollipop lady and crossed the road. School was just ten minutes away.

'I keep getting this falling dream,' explained Tom. 'And when it wakes me up there's a white figure in my bedroom, a ghostly white figure of a young girl.'

'A white figure?' repeated Beefy. 'That's not normal, Tom. Normal people dream about food.'

They passed through the school gate and

into the playground. Melissa Morgan and a group of her friends were practising a dance as the boys walked across the yard and stood near the wall. Melissa glanced across and gave Tom a flashing smile.

'Last night was my strangest dream yet,' continued Tom, turning his back to Melissa. 'I was in a forest watching myself as a young child. The whole family was there, Mum, Dad and Serena. We'd had a picnic and mum lost her ring. It caught on the picnic cloth and flew up into the air. I stood at the edge of the forest clearing and watched it turn and spin in the sunlight and then land on the forest floor in amongst the pine needles.'

Chris looked worried. Tom had a glazed look on his face as he recounted his dream. Beefy just stood there with his mouth open.

'When we had left the clearing – the family, I mean – in my dream, I walked forward and picked up the ring. That's when I saw the figures.'

'The figures?' repeated Beefy. 'What figures?'

'They were children,' explained Tom. 'Two boys and a girl. They were all dressed the same and they had been watching from amongst the trees. Anyway, they came into the clearing and they spoke to me.'

'What did they say?' asked Beefy. His eyes were growing wider by the second.

'They said they were friends,' replied Tom. 'They said they really needed to talk to me and that

I was to go back and meet them again tonight.'

'Are you going to go?' said Beefy eagerly. 'Are you going to meet them again?'

'How can I?' replied Tom. 'It was only a dream, wasn't it?' He decided to leave out the bit about waking up with the ring in his hand.

'I think you should see a doctor,' said Chris, emphatically. 'I've never heard such a load of rubbish in all my life!'

'Just one more thing I want to ask,' said Beefy, his eyes wide in anticipation. 'What did you have in your picnic?'

Tom had no chance to respond. The school bell rang and the children hurried to their lines in readiness to begin a new school week.

Monday afternoon meant history for Year 6. Tom had always liked history. He was fascinated by the past and he had always been able to imagine what it must have been like to live in bygone times. As the teachers talked he would see pictures in his mind and, sometimes, he even imagined he heard the voices of people from the past. Mrs Howarth, Tom's class teacher, brought history to life and after registration, Tom got out his books and waited eagerly for the lesson to begin.

The Year 6 class was studying the Tudors and Stuarts. The children had already learned about King Henry VIII and his six wives and they had just completed a unit about the Spanish Armada. However, it was the next unit that Tom was really looking forward to.

'We're going to learn about The Great Plague,' began Mrs Howarth and the children sat up immediately, the boys looking particularly interested. 'It was also known as The Black Death and, although it had been present in Britain for centuries, it struck London with a vengeance in the year 1665.'

Chris Edwards nudged Tom and whispered, 'This is going to be great! Dead bodies everywhere!'

Melissa Morgan screwed up her face in disgust.

'Now, before we talk about the plague itself, we need to know a little bit about Stuart London and the conditions that contributed to the spread of the plague.'

Mrs Howarth went on to explain how the poorest people of London lived in squalor. She told the children about the wooden houses crammed together and about the filthy streets, littered with rubbish and waste that had been thrown out of windows or dumped out of doors. She tried to get them to imagine the stray dogs and the cats and the rats that infested the streets and houses. She talked about the smell; the smell of the people who couldn't wash properly and had no change of clothes; the smell of the streets, piled high with rotten, decaying rubbish. Even Chris Edwards was pulling a face by the time Mrs Howarth had finished – and Melissa's complexion had turned a delicate shade of green.

'Now, I want you to watch a video,' continued Mrs Howarth. 'It will give you a really good idea as to what life was like in Stuart London.'

The teacher flicked a switch to turn off the classroom lights and she pressed the start button on the remote control. It was such a dull day outside that the room was quite dark and the children sat in silence in the gloom waiting for the programme to begin. Tom leaned forward, placed his elbows on the table and rested his head in his hands. His eyes were firmly fixed on the T.V. screen. The introductory music sounded and the titles began to roll.

Surprisingly, the programme started with a group of young children playing in a schoolyard. It was the present day and the sun was shining brightly above the modern school. The children were holding hands and moving around in a small circle. Tom recognised the rhyme they were singing:

> 'Ring - a - ring of roses,
> A pocketful of posies,
> Atishoo! Atishoo!
> We all fall down!'

As they chanted the last line, the children tumbled to the ground and the scene on the T.V. screen began to fade to be replaced by one of Stuart London. It was distant, at first, with the title imposed over the view but the camera gradually closed in to show a bustling market scene.

'The Year is 1665,' began the commentator.

His voice was deep and serious. 'The City of London is in the grip of a terrible plague and the people are filled with panic. Many have tried to escape but the City gates have been closed in an attempt to stop the spread of the plague. The narrow streets and the filthy conditions ...'

Tom was mesmerised. He stared at the T.V. screen as the images appeared before him. The camera moved away from the market scene and focused on a cobbled street that was littered with rubbish and filth. It spilled from the doorways and completely blocked the rough channel that ran down the centre of the road. The houses were jammed tightly together, badly built wooden constructions that overhung the street and let in little light. It was strange. Tom felt as if he was there, standing at the entrance to the street, staring at the disorder and the disease infested rubbish.

As the camera moved forward, Tom was drawn into the street, which seemed strangely quiet after the busy market place. The first few doors at the top end of the street were open. A woman, dressed in tattered clothes, was sitting at the entrance nursing a crying child. Several other ragged children stood behind her and stared out into the street, their thin faces smudged and dirty. Three bony cats were scavenging for scraps in the gutter, their fur matted and mangy. Tom could hear a dog barking and a man shouting and cursing in the distance.

19

Tom seemed to move further into the street and he was suddenly aware of the smell, the disgusting, dreadful smell of rotting, decayed food and human waste. There was an awful taste in his mouth and when Tom tried to swallow he almost choked. Suddenly, there was a clatter above his head as a window flew open and he glanced up just in time to see a woman lean out. She flung the contents of a large bowl into the air and the slops cascaded to the street below, causing Tom to leap to one side to avoid being drenched. One of the cats wandered over and began to lick up the mess.

Tom was conscious that something strange was happening. He moved forward again, slowly picking his way through the dirt and rubbish. The street seemed to be getting narrower and darker, the houses even closer together, as if they were pressing in on him. And then, in the gloom, Tom saw something that made his blood run cold. As he looked down the street, a ghostly white figure appeared at the far end. Tom knew immediately that it was the young girl, the same young girl who had appeared at the end of his falling dream. Tom watched in disbelief as the figure turned slowly and walked away before fading from view. The very next moment, a wailing, moaning sound split the air and Tom stopped and turned his head towards the dreadful noise. It sounded like a woman crying out in pain and it seemed to be coming from behind a closed door. As Tom stared at the door in horror, he let out a gasp and a shiver of fear ran through his whole body. The rotting wooden door was daubed with a red cross and the words 'Lord have mercy upon us' were roughly painted underneath. Tom recoiled in disbelief as the images before him seemed to swirl and fade and the words of the familiar rhyme grew louder and louder in his mind:

'Ring - a - ring of roses,
A pocketful of posies,
Atishoo! Atishoo!
We all fall down!'

Suddenly, there was a flash of light and Tom jerked bolt upright in his chair. He was dazed and confused and he could hear a familiar voice.

'And so you see the words of the nursery rhyme have a sinister meaning.'

It was Mrs Howarth. She was standing beside the television set addressing Year 6.

'The ring of roses refers to the red blotches that appeared on the skin. They were a sure sign that the bubonic plague had struck. People believed that the smell from a pocket full of posies would overpower the germs. Of course, that was not the case and once the victim started sneezing, death was not too far away. *Atishoo! Atishoo! We all fall down!'*

Gemma Jones stuck her hand up and waved it in the air. 'Please, Miss, Melissa says she feels sick!'

'Oh, dear! She does look a bit green!'

agreed Mrs Howarth. 'Take her to the door for a breath of fresh air, will you, Gemma. I'm sure that will do the trick.'

'Perhaps she's got the plague, Miss,' suggested Beefy, as Melissa shuffled past with her hand over her mouth. 'She looks a bit black around the eyes.'

'Thank you, Brian – but you can't catch The Black Death from a television set! I'm certain that she'll recover in a few minutes.'

It was then that Mrs Howarth noticed Tom. He was still sitting bolt upright in his place but his hands were shaking and his lips were quivering. Beads of sweat had broken out on his forehead.

Mrs Howarth approached him with a worried look on her face. 'Thomas? Are you all right, Thomas? Do you want to join Melissa for a breath of fresh air?'

The suggestion seemed to do the trick. Tom shook his head and sat back in his seat.

'No ... no thanks, Mrs Howarth. I'll be fine. I didn't sleep very well last night. I'm a bit tired. That's all it is.'

'Well, if you're quite sure,' said the teacher, backing away. 'You've turned very pale, Thomas. Anyone would think you'd seen a ghost!'

Chapter 3

The Friends

Tom couldn't get to sleep. He had done all the right things before going to bed. He had wallowed in a hot bath, he had made himself a milky drink and a piece of hot, buttered toast, he had sat up in bed and read a good book for half an hour before settling – but he just could not get to sleep. The problem was that he desperately wanted to get to sleep, to fall into his dream and return to the strange, silent forest to visit his friends – but his mind was so active that sleep was impossible.

Tom lay there in the darkness and his thoughts drifted back to the television programme he had watched earlier at school that afternoon. For Tom it had been frighteningly realistic, just like his meeting in the forest with the three mysterious children. Yet on the way home when he had talked about the experience to Chris and Beefy, it was as if they had watched a different programme.

'White figure?' Chris had said, looking surprised. 'What are you talking about, Tom? There was no white figure drifting around a street. In fact, I don't even remember the street you're describing.'

Beefy nodded his head in agreement. 'Perhaps it was a reflection on the T.V. screen,' he suggested. 'Perhaps a bit of sunlight had filtered into the room and it was reflecting on the screen.'

'It was raining,' snapped Tom. 'There was no sunlight on the screen. It was the same white figure that appeared in my bedroom after my falling dream. It was really there. I saw it just before the woman started to moan and the camera closed in on the wooden door with the red cross.'

Chris and Beefy exchanged worried glances.

'Moaning sound?' repeated Chris, slowly. 'And a wooden door with a red cross? That wasn't in the programme either, Tom. The programme was about living conditions in Stuart London. Mrs Howarth said that the next programme would explain all about the bubonic plague.'

Tom couldn't understand it. He had seen the figure, he had heard the awful moaning and, more worryingly, his senses had been attacked by the disgusting smells of the filthy street. He tossed and turned in his bed and he didn't understand.

Tom glanced at his bedside clock. An hour had passed and he was still awake. He got up to go to the toilet and there was Serena, in the bathroom, standing in front of the mirror dabbing a white cream onto her face.

'What's that?' asked Tom, doing his best to stifle a giggle. His sister's face was covered in white blotches.

'It's my spot cream,' said Serena, holding up the tube. 'Go away and leave me in peace.'

'Well it certainly works,' said Tom. 'Your

face is covered in spots!'

Serena flung a damp flannel at him and Tom darted out of the bathroom just in time. He still needed the toilet but he could wait another ten minutes.

Tom climbed back into bed and sighed deeply as he closed his eyes in a determined effort to drift into sleep. Gradually, his breathing became slower and heavier and his thoughts became more confused. Strange images began to float through his mind. Tom was aware that the images were all mixed up and mingled together. He saw Beefy tucking into a huge mountain of food. Beefy had a giant knife and fork in his hand and he was cramming the food into his mouth so that it dribbled and dropped from his chin onto his stained clothes. He saw Mrs Howarth standing before the class, her clothes ragged, her eyes staring, red blotches covering her face – and then the face turned into Serena's and it was bursting with big red spots that were topped with a white cream that looked like shaving foam. He saw Melissa Morgan performing a grotesque tap dance. Her blonde curls were longer than ever and her face was glowing green so that it cast a ghostly glow on the ground below. And then, suddenly, he was falling, spinning and turning in the darkness, brief familiar images flashing through his mind.

Somehow it was different this time. Tom was aware of his falling dream and he felt more in control. He was aware that he was beginning to enjoy the sensation. He knew where he wanted to be. He wanted to be in the forest clearing and it was almost as if he was willing the dream to take him there. After a while, the spinning sensation seemed to slow down and, when Tom opened his eyes, he was there, standing all alone at the edge of the forest clearing.

He stood for a moment and he looked and he listened. There was no sound – perhaps just a faint rustling of leaves in the light breeze. He hadn't noticed that before. There was definitely a light breeze. He glanced up towards the roof of the forest and he could just about see the sky through the leaves and the branches, fluffy white clouds drifting against a pale blue background.

Tom took a few paces forward towards the fallen tree trunk that had provided a seat for the mysterious boy. He could sense that he was being watched and he felt uncomfortable. He scanned the edge of the clearing and then he spoke, hesitantly:

'Hello! Is there anybody there? I've come back to see you as you asked.'

There was a movement to Tom's right and the mysterious boy who had spoken to him in his last dream stepped into the clearing. The girl was there, too, and the sullen boy, just a few steps behind her.

'We knew you'd come back,' said the first boy. 'We were confident you'd manage to find us.'

'I really don't understand,' said Tom. 'Who are you? Where have you come from?'

The boy indicated towards the fallen tree trunk. 'Come and sit down,' he said. 'I told you we needed to talk to you.'

Tom moved forward and perched on the makeshift seat. The two boys joined him, one on either side and the girl with the golden hair sat down cross-legged on the forest floor.

'I think you've realised that you're not the same as everyone else,' began the first boy. 'You're one of us, Tom. That's why you're here in the forest.'

'What are you talking about?' said Tom, indignantly. 'Of course I'm the same as everyone else. I know I'm adopted, if that's what you mean. I know I'm not living with my real parents and I know Serena isn't my real sister, thank goodness!'

'That's not what we mean,' said the golden haired girl. 'Lots of children are adopted. That doesn't make you special.'

'You're special because you're here, now, with us,' explained the first boy. 'I'm Marcus, this is Rosie and this is Carlos. You've travelled through time and you're here with us.'

Tom's face looked ashen. His mouth opened but, for a few moments, no words came out.

'Travelled through time,' he repeated, slowly. 'What do you mean *travelled through time?*'

'It's obvious,' said Rosie. 'I'm surprised

you hadn't realised. How else could you be there, watching your own family when your mother lost her ring. You knew that event happened years ago.'

'But ... but ... I was dreaming,' stammered Tom. 'You can see things that have already happened in a dream, you know.'

'Then how do you explain taking the ring back with you?' asked Marcus. 'It was there, in your hand, when you woke up, wasn't it Tom?'

'Yes, it was there,' agreed Tom, and he held his hand out and looked down at his palm, as if expecting to see the golden ring.

'We know all about you,' said Rosie, softly. 'We've been waiting for you, Tom. We were told to expect you and to look out for you.'

'Why would you want to look out for me?' asked Tom.

Rosie and Marcus exchanged a nervous glance.

'I told you, we're your friends,' said Marcus. 'Travellers have to look out for each other. Time is full of dangers and it would be easy for a new traveller to get into trouble.'

Tom appeared to be satisfied with the answer and the two friends seemed relieved.

'But how do you become a time traveller?' asked Tom. 'Can anyone learn to travel through time? Will I be able to bring my friends to meet you?'

There was a sneering laugh to Tom's left.

'Don't be ridiculous! Of course you can't bring your friends. It's not some sort of club, you know!'

It was the first time the sullen boy had spoken and Rosie and Marcus glared at him.

'Take no notice of Carlos,' said Rosie. 'He can be a bit grumpy at times.'

Carlos scowled, jumped up from the tree trunk and stomped off towards the edge of the forest clearing, kicking at the ground as he did so.

'He's always suspicious of new travellers,' said Rosie, as way of explanation.

'You don't learn to become a time traveller,' said Marcus, 'you are born a time traveller. You were born in a leap year, Tom, on the twenty-ninth of February. You share the same birthday as Rosie, Carlos and myself – and lots of other time travellers. We were all born on the twenty-ninth of February.'

'Of course, you've got to learn to control your ability to time travel,' continued Rosie. 'Lots of people have the ability to time travel but only a few ever use it.'

Tom thought for a moment and then he said, 'Are you asleep at the moment, like me? Have you fallen into time?'

'We live here in the forest,' replied Rosie, 'but not necessarily in this time. There are caverns and caves but it's not safe for us to stay in the one time for too long.'

'Don't you have any parents?' asked Tom.

'Aren't you even adopted, like me? Who looks after you?'

'We look after each other,' replied Marcus. 'We're very good at looking after each other – and there is always someone we can turn to for advice.'

Tom thought again. There was so much he did not understand. 'But am I asleep or am I really here?' he asked. 'I can't be in two places at once!'

'Yes, you can,' said Marcus. 'You're asleep and you're really here. Sleep is a door into the unconscious world. When you fall asleep you fall into time. You must have had that sensation, Tom, spinning and turning and falling through never ending space. Most people wake up suddenly and the sensation is broken but you can control it, Tom. You can fall into time and visit people and places from the past.'

'So you can only time travel when you're asleep?' said Tom.

'Of course you can't only time travel when you're asleep!' snapped Carlos. 'Don't you know anything about time?' He had wondered back over to the fallen tree trunk and he was picking at the soft bark, tearing pieces off and throwing them across the clearing.

Rosie frowned at the surly boy and turned her attention back to Tom. 'Sometimes, if you close your eyes, or even if you just concentrate really hard, you can almost feel yourself falling into time. Have you ever done that, Tom? Have you ever felt yourself time travelling?'

31

'Yes, I think I have,' said Tom, slowly. He was remembering the television programme and the strange, realistic feeling he had experienced of being drawn into the London street. 'A door into the unconscious world,' repeated Tom. 'A time door.'

'That's right,' confirmed Marcus, 'and you can learn to take control so that you can travel through time and visit wherever and whenever you want. It's not an easy thing to do. It takes a lot of practice but I've got a feeling you will make a good traveller, Tom.'

'And when I come out of it, when I've finished travelling, I'll still be there in bed or at my desk in school.' Tom was beginning to understand. 'It's quite simple really, isn't it?'

'Well, it's not that simple,' said Marcus, slowly. He stood up and walked around the fallen trunk, Tom's eyes following him all the way. 'You see, you are in real danger, Tom. That's why we were so eager to talk to you. We couldn't just leave you wandering the forest on your own. The Time Master sent us to find you so that we could take you to him. He needs to warn you about the danger.'

Tom looked incredulous. He started to laugh, a false, nervous laugh that faded quickly into a worried frown.

'The Time Master?' he repeated. 'What are you talking about? Who on earth is The Time Master?'

Tom shivered, suddenly. The light breeze had changed and it was blowing stronger and colder, picking up the fallen leaves from the forest floor and causing them to twist and swirl. The three friends noticed it, too and they exchanged worried glances.

'We must leave at once,' said Marcus, anxiously and he took hold of Tom's arm as if to encourage him to move quickly.

The wind picked up even more. It rushed through the tree tops so that the frantic branches swayed and beat against each other.

'Leave?' repeated Tom, rising from the fallen tree trunk. 'What's happening? Why have we got to leave?'

'You don't understand,' shouted Marcus. 'Hemlock's coming! He's already entered the forest! We've got to move quickly, Tom! We've got to escape!

Chapter 4

The Time Master

Tom sensed the urgency in Marcus's voice and he leapt from the fallen tree trunk, ready to follow him into the forest. Carlos had already disappeared and Rosie was waiting anxiously at the edge of the clearing.

'Come on!' urged Marcus. 'Keep close to Rosie. The path isn't easy. I'll stay at the back to make sure you don't get left behind!'

Rosie left the clearing and started along the narrow forest track. She was quick and agile and, more importantly, she knew exactly where she was going. She raced ahead like a forest deer. Tom struggled from the start. The track was overgrown with roots and ferns and Tom, gripped with fear, stumbled along in the semi-darkness. Marcus coaxed and encouraged him and somehow he kept going, his eyes focusing on Rosie's golden hair that seemed to be disappearing further and further into the distance.

The path was so overgrown that at one point it became like a tunnel, so that the children had to crouch low to pass through. Branches snatched and snagged at Tom's clothes and brambles grasped and tore at his ankles. Overhead, the wind howled and the branches whipped and lashed madly, as if fighting each other for space.

Eventually, the track widened again and the children emerged into a wider clearing. Ahead, the rocky land rose steeply, still forested, stretching away into the distance as far as the eye could see.

Tom staggered into the clearing and collapsed to the ground, gasping for breath. He closed his eyes and took in deep gulps of air and, when he opened them again, he saw Carlos directly in front of him, sitting on top of a huge boulder, staring at him suspiciously. The wind had dropped and the forest was becoming calmer by the second.

'Are you all right, Tom?' It was Rosie who spoke. She was not in the least bit out of breath.

'I think so,' replied Tom. 'What was all that about? Who on earth is Hemlock?'

Marcus and Rosie looked at each other nervously. Even Carlos turned his head away at the mention of Hemlock's name.

Marcus sat down on the forest floor next to Tom. His face was serious. 'Hemlock,' he said, slowly, 'is our bitter enemy. Make no mistake, Tom, Hemlock is your enemy. He will know that a new traveller has arrived in the forest and he will come after you. He was close behind us in the clearing.'

'If he knows so much, why didn't he follow us along the forest track? He can't be much of an enemy if he gives up so easily!'

'You stupid boy!' snapped Carlos, jumping down from his position on the boulder. 'Everyone knows what Hemlock is like! If he catches you, you'll never be seen again!'

Tom glared at Carlos. He really didn't like the sullen boy who seemed so rude and abrupt.

'The caves are over here, in the hillside,' explained Marcus. 'Hemlock won't follow us to the caves. He won't take on The Time Master.'

Marcus stood up and reached out a hand to help Tom to his feet. 'Come on,' he said. 'He's expecting you. We'll take you to meet The Time Master.'

The entrance to the cavern was half way up the wooded hillside. It was not a difficult climb. A gentle track wound upwards through the trees, much wider than the one that had formed their escape route from Hemlock. The children ascended in silence, Marcus leading the way, Tom aware that something momentous was about to happen.

Suddenly, Marcus veered off the main path and took a side track. It was a little narrower but it was still easy to negotiate. After about fifty metres he stopped by a rocky outcrop. An ancient, gnarled tree that seemed to hang in mid air and twist and turn to the ground caught Tom's attention. Its massive roots were embedded into the rock and it was scarred and stripped of bark. It looked as if it had been struck by lightning, not once but several times, so that it was in the last throes of life.

Tom stared at the tree in amazement. He had never seen anything like it – not even in his dreams.

'It's there,' said Marcus, nodding towards the old tree.

Tom looked puzzled and then he saw the opening in the rock face, disguised by the tangle of branches. Somehow, Tom had expected a huge open cave, like the ones he had found on the beach when he had been on holiday in Cornwall – but it wasn't like that. It was more a narrow crevice between two huge slabs of rock. It was as if the rock face had split open and created an entrance to the craggy hillside. Perhaps it had been split open by the same lightning strike that had shaped the old tree.

Carlos was the first to enter. He scrambled over and between the bare branches and disappeared into the hillside. The others followed. Tom didn't like it. The entrance itself was narrow but the stone walls soon closed in further making the passage dark and claustrophobic. It was damp, too. Droplets of water dripped from the low roof and trickled down the walls making the passage wet and slippery. Tom edged his way forward, his hands on the rough side walls to steady himself.

'I can see why Hemlock won't follow you here,' he joked, but his voice betrayed the nervousness he felt inside.

Suddenly, the passage widened and the children stepped out into a vast cavern. It was awesome. Tom could see it clearly, for it was lit by a number of lamps that had been carefully positioned around the walls. They were the sort of lamps Tom had seen in his history books. He could remember a sepia brown picture of Florence Nightingale holding such a lamp. The great cavern stretched before him and Tom stared into its vastness. He shivered in the cold, damp air and he turned to the three friends in anticipation.

'Is this it?' he whispered. 'Is this where I'll meet The Time Master?'

Even though he spoke in a whisper, his voice echoed eerily around the cavern. The Time Master … The Time Master … Meet the time Master …

'We're nearly there,' confirmed Carlos. 'Follow me.' It was the first time Carlos had taken the lead.

The children kept to the edge of the cavern where a smooth path seemed to have been worn into the rock. There were stalactites and stalagmites, some of which had joined together to form columns and there were weird shaped rocks that had been weathered over the centuries. There were several more crevices in the rock wall, passages that led away from the great cavern into the heart of the rocky hillside. It was through one of these crevices that Carlos disappeared, pausing briefly to beckon the others to follow.

'Go on,' said Rosie, as Tom hesitated. 'Follow Carlos. We're nearly there.'

Tom squeezed through the narrow gap, which opened almost immediately into a much smaller cavern, also lit by several lanterns. Rosie and Marcus joined him and the four children stood silently in the empty cavern. Tom took a couple of steps forward and looked around. It was about the size of Tom's classroom at school – perhaps just a bit bigger – but it couldn't have been more different. The roof was quite low and it was damp, just as the great cavern had been. There seemed to be shelves hewn out of the rock and it was on these shelves that the lanterns had been placed, their flickering lights casting an eerie, orange glow. Directly opposite the entrance there was a table, roughly carved out of the rock and there was a great stone slab that Tom guessed served as a seat. A loose cover was thrown over part of the seat and there were some dishes and plates on the table, old dishes with a delicate blue pattern around the edge, the sort of dishes his grandma kept in the china cabinet. There was a pile of books on the floor, to the side of the seat. They were old, too and they looked as though the damp had damaged them.

Tom took it all in quickly and then he turned back to the friends and said, 'There's no one here. I thought you were bringing me to meet The Time Master?'

Not one of the friends answered. Instead, they looked beyond Tom, over his shoulder towards the stone seat. Tom turned again and his heart missed a beat. A tall figure was standing perfectly still in front of the stone slab, his body outlined in the orange glow, his face swathed in shadow. He seemed to have appeared from nowhere and Tom blinked to make sure that his eyes were not deceiving him

Tom took a few hesitant paces forward

and stared at The Time Master. He was not at all as Tom had expected. He had imagined an old man with white flowing hair and a white beard and, on seeing The Time Master, Tom's first reaction was one of disappointment. He looked quite ordinary. He had scruffy black hair and he looked as if he needed a shave; he wore a sloppy jumper with denim jeans and a pair of battered trainers. He was dressed, in fact, exactly the same as the friends.

Nobody spoke for a few moments until The Time Master broke the silence.

'You must be young Thomas, I presume. I'm pleased to meet you, Thomas Travis.'

His voice was deep and precise.

'I'm pleased to meet you, Sir.' Tom didn't know what to call The Time Master. He didn't feel nervous anymore, just curious.

The Time Master sat down on the stone slab and he indicated to the floor in front of him. 'Come and sit down, Thomas. Marcus, Carlos, Rosie – why don't you join us.'

The children moved forward and perched on the floor in front of the stone slab.

'How was your journey?' asked The Time Master. 'Not too troubled, I hope?'

Tom thought for a moment. Did he mean his journey through time to the forest or did he mean the journey to the time cavern? After a short pause Tom replied, 'It was fine, thanks. No trouble at all.'

'And you've met our friends, here,'

continued The Time Master, indicating towards the children. 'You always need friends, Tom, no matter where you are in time. These friends will never let you down.'

Tom smiled politely and felt awkward.

The Time Master leaned forward and clasped his hands together. He stared down at the ground for what seemed like an eternity. Tom could hear the steady drip of water somewhere towards the back of the cavern. Eventually, The Time Master raised his head and looked directly into Tom's eyes.

'You should know, Thomas, that you are a very special person. I know you are special and the friends know you are special – and unfortunately Hemlock knows you are special.'

'I guess I'm very lucky,' said Tom, although he didn't feel particularly lucky at that moment. 'I don't think any of my friends can time travel. Wait until I tell them about it!'

'You should tell no one,' said The Time Master, his voice raised in concern. 'You were born in a time, Tom – that's your time – but you can travel through time. That is a wonderful power to have – but it is also a very dangerous power to have and you are in more danger than anyone, because you share *the secret*.'

'*The secret*?' repeated Tom. 'What are you talking about?'

'Hemlock is desperate to capture *the secret*, Tom. He is the enemy of all the friends but he is especially your enemy because he knows you share *the secret*. You must avoid Hemlock at all costs. Do you understand me?'

'I understand, Sir,' said Tom. 'But what is *the secret*? And who do I share it with? I can hardly give Hemlock *the secret* if I don't know what it is, can I?'

'I can't tell you any more at the moment,' said The Time Master, shortly. 'You don't need to know, yet. It will be safer for you if you don't know about it.'

'You mean it's a secret!' said Tom, and he chuckled quietly at his own joke.

The Time Master was not amused. His piercing blue eyes widened and he stared hard at Tom. 'Hemlock is your bitter enemy,' he repeated. 'Forget that simple fact and it could cost you dearly. Avoid Hemlock and his followers at all costs.'

'Has the secret got anything to do with ghosts?' persisted Tom.

The Time Master's expression stiffened. He threw a nervous glance towards the friends and he sat upright on the stone slab.

'Ghosts?' he repeated. 'Why do you ask about ghosts, Thomas?'

'It's just that when I came out of my dream the other night, there was a white figure in my room. I've never really believed in ghosts but I'm sure I didn't imagine it. There was the ghostly white figure of a young girl at the foot of my bed.'

The Time Master looked agitated. 'How many times have you seen the figure?'

'I think I saw her again in the street,' said Tom. 'We were watching a programme about The Great Plague at school and it was almost as if I was there. It was so realistic. I could even smell the street. And she was there, at the far end of the street, the same white figure.'

'It's not a ghost, Tom – it's a message.' The Time Master's voice had lowered to a whisper. 'The young girl is a fellow traveller, Tom and she is in trouble. She is looking for help, Tom – and she needs you to help her.'

'But I don't understand,' said Tom. 'Who is she? Why would she choose me to help her?' He stared in bewilderment at The Time Master and then at the friends and then back to The Time Master. 'After all,' he continued, 'you're far more experienced travellers than me. Why doesn't she turn to one of you for help?'

'You must leave me to consider the problem,' replied The Time Master, rising from his stone seat. 'You must travel back to your time, Tom and get on with your life. Soon, very soon, you will return to the forest. I will be there waiting for you. The friends will be there, too. We'll talk again then, Tom.'

'How can I get on with my life?' said Tom,

in some irritation. 'You can't just leave it at that. I want to know more about you all.' He turned to face the friends – but there was no one there.

Something strange was happening. The light from the lanterns was dimming and the cavern was becoming darker and darker. Tom spun back round to face The Time Master only to find that he, too, had disappeared. Tom suddenly felt dizzy. His head was spinning in the darkness. He tottered for a moment and then reached out a hand to steady himself. It was no use. He was falling ... falling ... spinning and turning in the pitch darkness ... falling ... falling ...

Chapter 5

Hideaway House

It was so frustrating. It had been a whole week since the friends had taken Tom to see The Time Master and he was beginning to doubt that it had ever happened at all. He had woken up the next morning even more grumpy than usual. He had snapped at Serena and left his breakfast untouched. He had even taken a longer route to school so that he didn't have to walk past Melissa Morgan's house or talk to his friends. That had made him late and he had got into trouble with Mrs Howarth. Still, it had been worth it not to have to listen to Beefy rambling on about mountains of food.

Even the history lesson had been a disappointment. Mrs Howarth had switched the videos on and Tom had prepared himself for a journey into the past – but it didn't happen. It just did not happen. Oh, the programme was interesting enough and Tom learned a lot more about the plague but there was no strange sensation of being drawn into Stuart London, he was in his seat in the classroom, with Melissa Morgan staring at him with wide, adoring eyes.

Night time, too, was frustrating. Tom desperately wanted to re-visit the forest and he had gone to bed early each night, determined to make the journey – but it just did not happen. He was asleep in no time, a deep dreamless sleep that took him right through to his alarm clock in the morning. It should have made him feel better, sleeping so well but instead, he was even more grumpy and irritable than normal.

It was exactly one week later, just as Tom was beginning to accept that the friends and The Time Master probably did not exist, that the next incident occurred to convince him otherwise.

It was a grey, murky Wednesday in mid February. It wasn't cold. A few weeks earlier it had snowed and the children had been allowed to play on the school field. That had been brilliant. Tom and his friends had pelted Melissa Morgan with snowballs and she had run off soaking wet to complain to the dinner ladies. The boys had got into trouble but it had been worth it! Now, however, the weather had returned to normal – damp, grey and boring.

Mrs Howarth had just blown her whistle for the end of lunchtime and the children were standing perfectly still in the yard. They were waiting for the second whistle, which was a signal for them to line up. Everything was perfectly calm and then, suddenly, a cold blast of wind gusted across the yard. It seemed to arrive from nowhere and the children shivered and glanced around at each other in surprise. At the same time, the sky darkened, the grey clouds gathering in a threatening, black mass.

Mrs Howarth looked concerned. She gave a shrill blast on her whistle.

'Move to your lines quickly, children. I think we could be in for a nasty storm.'

The wind was growing stronger as she spoke. It howled around the playground, whipping up the dust and the empty crisp packets that had escaped from the bins. A few of the younger children screamed and squealed as they hurried to their lines. Mrs Howarth, keeping an eye on the darkening sky, ushered them into school as quickly as possible.

It was Melissa Morgan who directed the teacher's attention to Tom. 'Mrs Howarth,' she whined, pointing across the yard, 'Thomas Travis hasn't come into his line. What's wrong with him, Miss?'

Mrs Howarth glared across at Tom, annoyed that it was one of her class who was keeping everyone waiting. Sure enough, he was there, standing on his own near the wall at the far side of the playground.

'Will you get a move on, Thomas Travis! What on earth do you think you're doing?'

There was no response. Tom stood absolutely still as if he was rooted to the spot. The wind howled around him yet he made no attempt to move. He seemed to be staring up into the sky, mesmerised by the gathering gloom.

'Thomas!' yelled the teacher. 'Get across here now!'

Still no response. The first huge droplets of rain fell from the leaden clouds. Mrs Howarth diverted her attention to the rest of the class.

'Go inside,' she ordered. 'Get your history books out ready for our lesson.'

Suddenly, a fork of silver lightning split the dark sky and a terrific crash of thunder followed almost immediately. Melissa Morgan screamed and Beefy's face turned as white as a sheet – but it galvanised Tom into action. He shook his head, looked all around and then dashed for the door, straight past the waiting children and the startled teacher.

'I'm sorry, Mrs Howarth,' said Tom, once they were settled in the classroom. 'I don't know what came over me. I just wasn't in control.'

'Yes, well thanks to you not being in control, Thomas Travis, the rest of us got a soaking. By the time we got into the building we were wet through!'

The rest of the class glared at Tom. Even Chris and Beefy looked angry. Only Melissa Morgan seemed to understand. She was sitting directly behind Tom. Her long blonde curls had taken a soaking and had turned so frizzy that she looked as if she'd had an electric shock. She leaned forward and whispered, 'It's all right, Tom. I don't mind that you weren't in control.'

Tom grimaced and stared straight ahead. What had he done? His only friend in the whole world was Melissa Morgan!

'Now then,' began Mrs Howarth, clasping her hands together. 'This has not been the best start to the afternoon but perhaps we can get on with our lesson.'

It was strange. The storm had completely passed. The weather was calm and the sky was its usual dull grey.

'This afternoon we're going to learn about a terrible disaster that happened in London in September 1666, just one year after the Great Plague. We will also learn that, although it was terrible at the time, some good came from the disaster. I am, of course, talking about The Great Fire of London.'

Tom wasn't paying attention. His mind was on other things. He felt ashamed that he had made a fool of himself in the playground and he just couldn't concentrate, even though it was his favourite subject. Once again, Mrs Howarth switched off the classroom lights and pressed the button on the remote control to start the video. The title credits rolled and, as the camera zoomed in on Stuart London, the narrator's deep and serious voice took control in the silent classroom.

'*It is the beginning of September in the year 1666. The Great Plague has taken its toll on the City of London. It has been a long, hot summer, one of the driest on record. The timber-framed buildings, packed closely together, overlook filthy streets where rubbish and waste has been left to rot in the heat. At his bakery in Pudding Lane, Thomas Farynor, the King's baker, is coming to the end of another busy day ...*'

Tom was staring out of the window. The dull grey winter clouds drifted overhead, heavy and oppressive but no longer threatening violence. Something was bothering him. There was something strange about the way the wind had suddenly swirled into the playground without any warning. Tom thought back to his experience in the forest clearing when the friends had urged him to flee from Hemlock. Surely there could not be a connection? Surely Hemlock would not venture into the present and seek him out at Hollow Lane School? Tom's eyes glazed over as the grey clouds drifted and swirled, forming dizzy patterns in the winter sky. The narrator's voice seemed to be somewhere at the back of his mind. He was feeling tired and confused and ashamed of the fuss he had caused. Tom closed his eyes for a few moments in an attempt to gather his thoughts and, when he opened them again, the clouds seemed to be all around him, like a choking, smothering fog.

Tom could hear voices, not the narrator or Mrs Howarth telling him to pay attention, frightened, desperate voices that shouted out in panic. The fog was stinging his eyes and grasping at the back of his throat causing him to splutter and cough. A sudden gust of wind cleared it for a moment and he stared in amazement at the scene of panic in the busy market place.

It took Tom seconds to realise that the fog was, in fact, smoke, choking black smoke that was whipped and driven by the strong, easterly wind. There were people everywhere, rushing past him in chaotic disorder; mothers clutching hold of bawling babies; men pushing carts laden with their belongings; children crying and looking around in desperation for lost parents; and all the time the choking smoke swirled and attacked.

Tom moved forward instinctively and a large, dishevelled man carrying a roughly tied bundle of clothes bumped into him, almost knocking him to the ground. A pathetically thin child who was no more than five years old was standing directly in front of him, wailing loudly. Tom was about to ask him what was wrong when a woman dressed in ragged clothes, her face dirty and smudged, snatched hold of the child and whisked it away.

Tom stumbled forward again, away from the confusion of the market place towards the narrow street where he had seen the cross on the door and the ghostly, white figure. As he entered the street, shouts of *Fire! Fire!* Were ringing in his ears. The street, too, was busy, far busier than the last time he had visited. People were hurrying in every direction, taking with them whatever they could carry. Tom seemed to be the only one who wasn't in a hurry. He walked slowly along the street, away from the market. It was still full of rubbish and waste but the acrid smoke that billowed overhead masked the smell.

A wooden door flew open and a woman rushed out carrying two blackened pots and a water jug. Seeing Tom, she paused for a moment and yelled at him.

'You must get away, boy! Get to the high ground or get down to the river before the fire strikes! You haven't got much time!'

Before he could reply, the woman had rushed away, dropping one of the pots in her haste to escape.

Tom glanced behind him to see deep red flames and showers of sparks leap into the blackened sky. The panic was catching and Tom felt a tremor of fear pass through his whole body. He turned his back on the distant flames and hurried along the street, not really sure what he was running from or where he was going. He took a right turn at the very end of the street as a group of people pushed past him, running in the opposite direction. This road was wider and he gathered speed, racing along the uneven cobbles, dodging the piles of rubbish that hindered his escape. His heart pounded and his breath came in gasps but he ran and ran until he could run no more. Tom sank to his knees beside a great stone wall and then he rolled over onto his back and stared up at the encroaching clouds of black smoke.

It was some minutes before Tom pulled himself up into a sitting position and, when he did so, he found himself staring at a battered wooden door that was set into the high stone wall. He realised that he had left the bustling streets behind him. There seemed to be a stretch of open heathland to the left of the stone wall, groups of people making their way over the open ground to escape the approaching fire, some of them pushing carts piled high with whatever they had been able to rescue from their threatened homes.

Tom stood up slowly. He was shaking and he wasn't sure why. After all, he was away from the immediate threat of the fire. He glanced around nervously and then turned back to face the wooden door. There was a faded sign on the stone wall beside the door. It was dirty and Tom rubbed it with the sleeve of his school jumper to reveal the words Hideaway House. Tom stared at the sign for a moment. Hideaway House. That must be the name of the building behind the wall. And it was hidden away. It stood all on its own, away from the busy streets bordering the heathland.

Tom noticed a latch half way down the door and he lifted it, expecting the door to be locked from the inside. To his surprise, it gave way at once, swinging inwards to reveal an expanse of overgrown garden.

Somewhere in the distance there was a loud boom and a huge flash of red flame leapt into the blackened sky. There were screams and cries and showers of sparks.

Tom stepped through the open door and

stood quietly inside the garden. He was aware that he was still breathing heavily. He could see the house at once, a huge Tudor House nestled amongst a clutch of trees at the end of a rough gravel driveway. The narrow path from the wooden door led directly to the driveway and Tom advanced, cautiously. At one time it had been a splendid house but it had clearly been neglected and it was in a state of disrepair. At first, Tom thought it was deserted but as he approached the driveway he noticed a faint light in one of the top windows. He stopped for a moment and stared up at the small leaded window set in the stone wall, wondering who was sheltering in this gloomy, mysterious building. The light in the window flickered, as if it was coming from a candle or an oil lamp. It reminded Tom of the flickering yellow glow that had been cast by the lamps in the time cavern.

There were more shouts in the distance and another shower of sparks exploded into the evening sky – but Tom felt strangely isolated inside the walled garden. It was as if the fire could not reach him.

Tom's attention was brought back to the house by a sudden movement in the upstairs room. Through the gloom, Tom could make out a figure at the window. It was a young girl, not ghostly white but solid and real. Although he was still some distance away, Tom could see her face, etched with

fear and desperation. He stood, frozen to the spot, as the girl spotted him on the path below and waved her arms frantically. Tom took a few steps forward until a booming, angry voice stopped him in his tracks.

'Hey! What are you doing 'ere? This is private property, 'ere!'

The voice belonged to a huge, brute of a man who had appeared from around the side of the house and was advancing threateningly in Tom's direction. His face was fearsome. He wore a black eye patch and a jagged purple scar zigzagged across his forehead from the damaged eye.

Tom didn't wait to take a closer look. He turned and ran for all he was worth, along the narrow footpath and straight through the wooden door.

Eye Patch was after him. 'Come 'ere yer rascal! I'll learn yer to break in Hideaway House!'

He was too late. Tom was off across the heath, leaping and bounding over the rough ground and tufts of grass. Once again, his heart was pounding and his lungs were bursting but he did not stop. He did not look back. He ran and ran and ran ...

Chapter 6

Visitor in the Night

There was a sudden crash in the classroom and the children sitting near to Tom jumped up in concern.

'He's fainted, Miss,' shouted Melissa Morgan, and she peered down at Tom with a worried expression on her face.

Mrs Howarth switched off the T.V. and hurried over to where Tom was lying in a crumpled heap.

'Move back, children. Let him get some air. Chris, will you open a couple of windows, please.'

'What's up with him, Miss?' asked Louise Wiggins. 'Why's he down there?'

Louise wasn't the brightest member of the class.

'He's obviously not very well,' explained Mrs Howarth, stooping down to take a closer look. 'That would explain his strange behaviour in the playground.'

'He's probably not had enough to eat,' suggested Beefy, helpfully. 'I go all faint when I haven't eaten enough.'

'That can't happen very often!' observed Chris.

'Will you move back, please!' snapped the teacher. 'Give him some room to breathe.'

Mrs Howarth leaned forward and shook

Tom's arm gently. 'Thomas? Can you hear me, Thomas? Are you all right?'

Tom moaned and moved ever so slightly. His eyelids flickered and he moaned again.

'He's all hot and sweaty,' observed Melissa. 'I don't like him like that!'

'Perhaps he's going to throw up,' observed Louise. 'My cat threw up this morning. I think it was something she'd eaten. It was all brown and sloppy and …'

'Be quiet, Louise!' commanded Mrs Howarth. 'Do something useful. Go and get Thomas a glass of cold water.'

Louise wandered off looking hurt.

'I've got a packet of crisps left if you think that would help,' offered Beefy. 'Prawn cocktail flavour.'

'Well, that's very kind,' said Mrs Howarth, doubtfully, 'but not just at the moment, Brian. I don't think Thomas could cope with prawn cocktail.'

Tom groaned and opened his eyes. He had no idea where he was. The first thing he saw was several pairs of shoes and this confused him even more. He moved his head slightly and realised that the shoes were connected to legs and that the legs belonged to his classmates.

'Thomas?' said Mrs Howarth, softly. 'Are you all right, Thomas? I think you must have fainted.'

'Yes – fainted,' repeated Tom. He made no

attempt to sit up. 'I was trying to get away from the house. He was running after me and I must have fainted.'

The other children giggled and nudged each other.

'I don't think anyone was running after you, Thomas,' said Mrs Howarth. 'You just fell off your chair. Would you like to try and sit up a little, Thomas?'

Mrs Howarth took hold of Tom's arm and helped him up into a sitting position, his back resting against the legs of a table. At that moment, Louise Wiggins returned carrying a disgusting looking plastic beaker full of cloudy water.

'It's all I could find, Miss,' she said, pushing her way past the watching children and thrusting the beaker forward.

'He can't drink that,' said Mrs Howarth, impatiently. That's one of the beakers we use to wash the paintbrushes. Take it away, Louise.'

Louise looked hurt. She crept away to the back of the class and sulked.

Tom was coming round and he was beginning to feel embarrassed. He was aware that everyone was looking at him. His cheeks, that only moments ago had a deathly white pallor, were beginning to be tinged with pink.

'He's getting better,' observed Melissa and she risked moving a little closer. 'He doesn't look all sweaty anymore.'

'He'll have a relapse if you move any closer!'

barked Beefy. 'Give him some space!'

Tom made an effort to stand up and Mrs Howarth helped him to his chair. He still looked a little dazed and he had no idea what had happened.

'I'm sorry, Mrs Howarth,' he said. 'I'm still not sleeping very well. I'll be all right now.'

'Yes, well I don't think we'll take any chances,' said the teacher. 'I think we'll send you home for the rest of the afternoon so that you can recover properly. Melissa, perhaps you could take Thomas to the school office. Explain what has happened and ask the secretary if she will be kind enough to ring Tom's mum.'

Melissa Morgan couldn't believe her luck. Her eyes widened and her whole face burst into a beaming smile.

Tom took one look at her and felt as though he were going to faint again.

'I don't know what all the fuss is about,' said Tom, as his mum ushered him through the front door and straight into the kitchen. 'I only fainted. Lots of people faint, you know.'

'You heard what the doctor said – hot drinks and plenty of rest. It's not natural, a boy of your age acting like that – and you've got a bump on the back of your head the size of an egg.'

His mum was exaggerating a little bit but there was a definite swelling and, in truth, Tom still felt a bit queasy. He couldn't get the image of the great brute with the eye patch out of his mind. He kept visualising him charging forward through a swathe of swirling black smoke. Tom sat at the kitchen table and watched as his mum switched the kettle on and reached for the teapot and two mugs.

'A nice cup of tea and then up to bed for a proper rest. We'll see how you are later. You might be all right to come down and watch a bit of television this evening.'

Tom's mum made awful tea. It always turned out bright orange and it left a mysterious film on the inside of cups and mugs. Tom took one look at it and felt very ill.

'I think I will have a lie down after all,' whimpered Tom. 'I'll take my tea upstairs with me.'

As soon as he had climbed the stairs, Tom darted into the bathroom and emptied his tea down the toilet. The very act of watching it flush away made him feel better. He took the empty mug into his bedroom and placed it next to his alarm clock on the small bedside table. Lying on the bed, Tom stared at the ceiling and wondered what on earth was happening to him. He had made a complete fool of himself at school, he knew that and yet he didn't care. He really wanted to be back in the forest with his mysterious friends. He wanted to talk to The Time Master and find out more about the ghostly young girl. Who was she? Why had she turned to him for help? Had he really seen her in the window of Hideaway House? Tom stared at the patterns on his ceiling and wondered if he would ever get to time travel again.

He was still staring at the ceiling when his sister burst into the room over an hour later. She had just arrived home from High School and she had rushed straight upstairs to torment him.

'Hello weirdo,' she said, peering down at him as he lay on the bed. 'What's all this about, then?'

'Go away. I'm not well.'

Tom rolled over onto his side so that he didn't have to look at his sister's sneering face.

Serena put on a silly voice and whined, 'That's not very nice when Serena's come in specially to comfort her little baby brother.' She bounced across to the bed and sat down on the end.

'I don't want any comfort,' snapped Tom. 'I'm not that ill.'

'You're not ill at all,' retorted Serena, poking his legs. 'You're just weird. I met Chris and Beefy on the way home from school. They think you're weird, too. They told me what happened today – rushing past everyone at dinnertime and then falling on the floor in a heap. You can't tell me that's not weird!'

'Leave me alone,' pleaded Tom. 'Go and tend to your spotty face!'

Tom had hit a nerve. 'I haven't got a spotty face!' insisted Serena, jumping up from the bed. 'You're getting more and more horrible! No one will want to talk to you! You won't have any friends because you're so weird!'

'You don't know anything,' snapped Tom,

rolling onto his back again. 'I've got plenty of friends – new friends that you don't know about.'

'You're lying!' said Serena, suspiciously. 'What new friends?'

'Secret friends,' said Tom in a hushed voice. 'Secret friends with secret powers.'

Serena said nothing for a moment. She stared hard at her brother, who had pushed himself up onto his elbows and was looking directly into her eyes. She held his gaze for a further few seconds and then said, 'Completely weird! You want locking away, you do!' And with that she turned and stomped out of the bedroom, slamming the door behind her.

Tom collapsed back down onto the bed and buried his face into the pillow. Straight away, he regretted having said anything about his 'secret friends', especially to his sister, Serena, who was sure to blurt it out to everyone she met. Why couldn't he learn to keep his big mouth firmly shut?

It was a long evening. Tom had eaten very little and he was beginning to feel hungry. Earlier, his mum had brought in his evening meal on a tray – poached yellow fish with mashed potato.

'This will do you the world of good,' she had explained, as Tom stared at it in disbelief. 'Whenever I was ill as a little girl, my mother always used to poach a nice piece of fish for me.' She put the tray down carefully on the end of his bed. 'I'll just leave it there for you and you can eat it in peace.'

'Thanks, mum,' said Tom, doing his best not to screw up his nose. 'That'll be great.'

The fish smelt awful. He wouldn't have given it to the cat, if he'd had one. Tom found a plastic supermarket bag in his sock drawer and he scraped his dinner into it as quickly as he could. He tied the neck tightly, crept to his bedroom door and peeped around it to see if there was anyone about. Seeing the coast clear, Tom darted into Serena's room and shoved the bag into the bottom of her wardrobe. He chuckled to himself as he imagined her investigating it in a few weeks time.

Tom's mum was delighted when she returned half an hour later to find an empty plate.

By 9 o'clock Tom was feeling exhausted. Too lazy to change into his pyjamas, he turned off his bedside lamp and crawled beneath the quilt. Outside, the weather was beginning to turn nasty. The wind had picked up and heavy rain beat down relentlessly but, somehow, it made Tom feel even more secure as he began to drift into sleep. Warm and comfortable beneath his quilt cover.

Tom began to dream almost immediately, not the falling, spinning dream that would take him to the Time Forest but a strange, mixed up dream that seemed to make no sense whatsoever. At first, he was crawling along amongst a sea of legs and then he was running for his life across a grassy heath. He turned to see Melissa Morgan chasing after him, her blonde curls blowing in the wind, her arms outstretched. Behind Melissa was Eye Patch, charging across the smouldering heath waving his fist in the air. Suddenly, Tom was enveloped in a cloud of choking smoke and when the smoke cleared, Beefy was standing in front of him eating a giant packet of prawn cocktail crisps. Beefy held the packet out and when Tom plunged his hand inside he pulled out a huge, yellow fish with one glazed, staring eye. The choking smoke descended again and Tom stumbled forward, screams of '*Fire! Fire!*' echoing around his head.

And then Tom was aware of another noise, a noise that seemed to be much closer, a noise that brought him out of his dream and sent a shiver of apprehension through his whole body. The wind was howling around the house, whistling through the trees and rattling the windows. Tom didn't move for a few minutes. He lay on his back listening to the storm, the quilt cover pulled over his face almost up to his eyes. He had no idea of the time. Outside, something crashed to the ground and shattered into pieces. Suddenly, Tom's curtains billowed inwards as the gale dislodged a latch and the window flew open. Tom felt the blast of cold air even though he was hiding beneath the cover. A pile of magazines and papers flew across the room as the latch rattled and the window banged open and shut.

Feeling scared, Tom slid out of bed and secured the latch. He peered out of the window into the darkness but he could see nothing other than the driving rain. He thought about calling for his mum but instead, he jumped back into bed and disappeared beneath his quilt.

Still the storm attacked, wave after wave of relentless rain battering at his bedroom window. It seemed to pause for a few minutes and then a tremendous clash of thunder signalled the next onslaught. Flashes of silver lightning lit Tom's room and the house seemed to be shaken to its foundations. Tom buried his head beneath the quilt, closed his eyes tight and put his hands over his ears. It seemed like an eternity before he came up for air and, when he did so, the lightning had stopped and the thunder was no more than a distant rumble.

Tom's room was plunged into darkness again and, for a few moments, he couldn't see a thing. Gradually, his eyes adjusted and Tom began to pick out various shapes. There was his clock on the bedside table and there was his school bag on the wicker chair in the corner. He looked across towards the door and there was his dressing gown hanging on its hook. Or was it? As Tom strained to see across the room his eyes widened in fear and, in an awful moment of realisation, he remembered that he no longer had a dressing gown. He had thrown it away before his birthday because it had become too small for him. There was someone in his room, moving ever so slowly forward from the shadows – and Tom was too scared even to cry out in terror.

Chapter 7

Back to the Time Cavern

Marcus stood at the end of Tom's bed and raised one finger to his lips as a signal for Tom to remain silent. In truth, Tom was so terrified that he couldn't have spoken even if he had wanted to. He sat there, cowered on his bed, his knees tucked up to his chin and he stared in disbelief as Marcus took a step closer.

'It's all right, he's gone now,' whispered Marcus. 'I don't think he'll try again for a while.'

'W-what are you talking about?' said Tom, his voice quivering with fear. 'Who won't try again?'

'Why, Hemlock, of course. You must have realised he's been trying to get to you. You've done well to fend him off.'

'Fend him off?' repeated Tom. 'Y-yes, yes – I remembered The Time Master's warning.'

Marcus moved forward again and sat down on the edge of Tom's bed. 'We've been waiting for you to return to the forest. She can't stay there forever, you know, Tom. Somebody will have to help her.'

Tom knew at once that Marcus was referring to the young girl who had first appeared to him as a ghostly white figure. He knew also that what Marcus said was true. The girl was in trouble. She needed help.

'I've tried to get back to the forest,' explained Tom. 'I've fallen asleep every night desperate to get back to the forest – but it hasn't happened. Why hasn't it happened, Marcus? What's gone wrong?'

'Nothing's gone wrong,' explained Marcus. 'It's Hemlock who's blocked your way. He doesn't want you meeting with us because he knows it would mean trouble for him. You'll be all right now. You must be very strong, Tom. He's tried his worst to get to you and he's failed. You'll be able to get through now. You'll be able to reach the forest. The Time Master will be waiting for you.'

'But what if I can't get to sleep?' questioned Tom. 'There's so much going around in my head.'

'You'll sleep,' said Marcus, reassuringly. He stood up and began to back away towards the door, further and further into the shadows. 'You'll sleep, believe me.'

Amazingly, Tom's eyelids were already feeling heavy. He tried to speak again but the words just would not come out. He gave in, allowing his head to sink in to the softness of his pillow. The wind no longer howled, the lightning no longer flashed and the thunder no longer crashed. With great effort, Tom stared into the darkness of his room but he saw nothing. Had Marcus really been there or had it been another strange illusion? The question echoed in Tom's head as he drifted into a deep, peaceful sleep.

Tom actually enjoyed the sensation. There was no feeling of desperation or fear as he twisted and turned and plunged down into the darkness of his dream. It was as if he wanted it to happen. He was in control and he wanted it to happen. He even recognised some of the faces that loomed out of the darkness. There was Serena as a child, selfishly snatching at him as he tumbled past; there was Mrs Jenkins, his first ever teacher, kind and smiling, just as he remembered her; and there was his grandma who had died when he was just two years old. Tom couldn't really remember her but he recognised her face from the picture that his mum kept on the dressing table in her bedroom. The falling sensation seemed to merge into a swirl of leaves and, as they began to settle, Tom realised that he was back in the Time Forest.

It was cold and a thin white mist hugged the forest floor. Tom shivered and put his arms to his shoulders. The forest was so still, so silent, so eerie. He looked around the clearing but there was no one there. The mist drifted around Tom's feet so that it seemed as if he was standing in a cloud. He looked down and felt a slight dizziness when he could not see the forest floor. Tom steadied himself and regained control and, when he looked up again, he was aware that he was no longer alone.

The Time Master was sitting on the fallen tree trunk staring steadily in Tom's direction and the three friends were standing behind him, their arms folded across their chests.

The Time Master was the first to speak.

'Well done, Tom! You made it! Marcus said you'd be joining us.'

Tom noticed that The Time Master was dressed exactly the same as the friends – a baggy, woollen jumper that looked two sizes too big for him and a pair of faded denim jeans. This wasn't at all like the science fiction books he'd read or the fantasy films he'd watched.

Tom took a few paces forward. 'I'm sorry it's taken me so long to return,' he said. He brushed his floppy hair away from his eyes with the back of his hand. 'I don't think I'm very good at time travelling. I-I had trouble sorting things out.'

'So long to return?' repeated The Time Master. 'Nonsense! Time means nothing, Tom, when you can control it. You can move through time whenever you choose. And that's what you're learning to do, Tom, you're learning to take control. Come and join me over here.'

The Time Master patted the tree trunk and Tom walked over and sat beside him.

'It's good to have you back,' said Rosie, and she placed a hand on Tom's shoulder, causing his cheeks to blush with colour.

'You're one of us, now,' added Marcus. 'You're one of our friends.'

Carlos remained silent, his arms folded firmly across his chest. It was just as well that Tom couldn't see the scowl on his sullen face.

'As you know, Tom, we've got a problem,'

began The Time Master. 'One of our kind is in deep trouble and has turned to you for help. It's a cry that cannot be ignored, Tom. We've got to do something about it.'

'I know that,' said Tom, quietly. 'I know we've got to do something about it.'

The Time Master looked uneasy. He glanced at Marcus and then placed a hand on Tom's arm. 'The young girl is Hemlock's prisoner, Tom. He's keeping her locked in time for a reason. You must realise that you will face great danger. You've got to journey into time and get her. You've got to bring her back here to the forest.'

Tom didn't say anything for a moment. He let The Time Master's words sink into his mind. He glanced at Rosie and Marcus and then he looked back to The Time Master.

'I don't understand why she's turned to me for help,' said Tom. 'And I don't understand why Hemlock would want to keep her prisoner. Why is she so important? Who is she?'

'You don't need to know that at the moment,' replied The Time Master. 'Hemlock has his reasons. Bring her back to the forest, Tom, and all will become clear.'

'When do I begin?' asked Tom. 'I don't know where to start.'

The Time Master once again placed a reassuring hand on Tom's arm. 'You won't be going alone,' he said. 'Marcus will travel with you. He's been on a mission before. You will bring the girl back together.'

'We're going soon,' continued Marcus. 'Hemlock's given up on you at the moment but you can be sure he'll be back to try again. We must travel before he realises what is happening.'

Tom gave a shiver of fear at the reality of his task. He didn't want to go; he knew he didn't want to go but there seemed no escape.

'Wh–what about my parents?' he stammered. 'They'll miss me! Even Serena will notice I'm missing! They'll panic when they realise I'm not there in the morning!'

'You will be there in the morning,' said The Time Master, reassuringly. 'Time travel doesn't work like that, Tom. No matter how long the mission takes you'll wake up back in your own bed in the morning. No one will miss you.'

Tom didn't understand but he nodded his head in submissive acceptance. 'How do we begin?' he asked. 'Surely we don't have to wait until we both fall into the right condition of sleep?'

'Of course not,' said The Time Master, rising from his position on the tree trunk. 'Experienced travellers go wherever and whenever they want. Marcus will take control but firstly we must return to the time chamber. Follow me, Thomas, and keep close – this mist is closing in.'

The journey seemed to take longer than Tom remembered, probably because they were not racing through the trees and undergrowth trying to escape from Hemlock. It was cold, bitterly cold and

Tom wished he had brought his fleece jacket. For the first time, he realised that he was not in his pyjamas. He had arrived in the time forest dressed the same as the friends. How could that happen? He shivered and thought again of his fleece. The friends didn't seem to feel the cold. Perhaps they were just used to it.

Eventually, they reached the hillside track that led up to the time cavern. There was the ancient, gnarled tree, blackened and disfigured by time. The Time Master paused for a moment and turned to face his followers.

'Where's Carlos?' he questioned, a concerned look on his face.

'He was right behind me,' explained Rosie, 'until a few minutes ago. Shall I go back and look for him?'

'Leave him!' snapped The Time Master, impatiently. 'He'll follow us into the caverns.'

The Time Master disappeared between the two huge slabs of rock that formed the entrance into the hillside. Tom, who was directly behind him, hesitated for a few moments. He had come to the conclusion that he was shivering more with fear than from the effects of the cold, swirling mist.

'Go on,' urged Marcus, sensing his anxiety. 'You'll be all right. The Time Master won't let anything happen to you.'

Tom smiled weakly and followed The Time Master through the narrow crevice into the dark passage.

They were in the cavern within minutes, the age old lamps casting their welcoming orange glow as they entered the vast space.

'Follow me,' whispered The Time Master, and hundreds of voices whispered back at him – 'Follow me ... Follow me ... Follow me ...'

The Time Master moved quickly, keeping to the worn rock path that wound its way around the edge of the great cave until he reached the narrow entrance to the smaller cavern. Tom wondered whether The Time Master would be able to squeeze through the tight gap but he passed through effortlessly, leaving Tom and the friends to struggle after him. By the time the children had entered the cavern, The Time Master was already seated on the huge, stone slab.

Tom was feeling more nervous by the minute and The Time Master sensed his anxiety.

'Come and join me,' he said, indicating for Tom to sit near him on the covered stone slab.

Tom edged forward hesitantly and sat down at the far end of the cold stone seat. The Time Master didn't speak for a moment. He leaned forward and stared at Tom, his piercing blue eyes unblinking as he concentrated. It was unnerving. Tom averted his gaze and he glared around the time cavern, taking in the flickering lamps that caused eerie shadows to dance across the stone floor. He noticed that Carlos had entered but he had not joined Marcus and Rosie. He was standing motionless against the far wall of the cavern, watching and waiting for The Time Master to give out his instructions.

'You must start your journey straight away. There is no time to lose, Tom.'

The Time Master's voice was serious and Tom turned back to face his stern glare.

'Does it matter when we travel?' asked Tom. 'If we can stop anywhere in time surely we can arrive before the girl is in danger?'

The Time Master gave a thin smile. 'Never underestimate Hemlock, Tom. If he knows the girl has made contact he will act on the information. He'll move her and she could be lost forever. Believe me, we have no time to lose.'

'But how do we know we'll arrive together?' persisted Tom. 'Marcus and me – how do we know we'll arrive at the right place and the right time?'

'Trust in Marcus,' replied The Time Master. 'He will be your guide. If you listen to him and do exactly what he says you will both be fine. You must find the girl and bring her back, Tom. It is imperative that she returns with you.'

'*The secret*,' said Tom, quietly. 'The girl shares *the secret*.'

'That's right,' confirmed The Time Master. 'The young girl shares *the secret*.'

Rosie stepped forward and placed her hand on Tom's shoulder. 'Good luck,' she said, softly. 'However long it takes we'll be waiting for you.'

Tom took a deep breath and closed his eyes. When he opened them again, The Time Master had gone, there was no comforting hand on his shoulder and Carlos had disappeared from his position against the far wall. Only Marcus remained and he stepped forward and sat next to Tom on the stone slab.

'Are you ready, Tom?'

'I – I think so,' replied Tom, hesitantly.

'Grasp hold of my hand and don't let go whatever happens.'

The moment Tom took hold of Marcus's hand the light from the lanterns began to flicker and fade. As the cold cavern darkened, Tom felt his head begin to spin. The dizziness increased and he reached out his free hand to steady himself but there was nothing there – only endless space. Tom was tumbling into the space, falling faster and faster through the endless darkness of time.

Outside the time cavern, the swirling mist had been driven away by a vicious wind that had penetrated the forest and was gnawing at the hillside. A single figure stood at the entrance to the cavern, his arms raised as if inviting the wind to rush through the narrow opening. Carlos cried into the wind before sinking to his knees and beating the ground in frustration.

Chapter 8

The Star Inn

Someone was calling Tom's name and shaking him roughly by the shoulder. Tom assumed it was his mother trying desperately to wake him up in time for school but, when he forced his eyes open, he saw Marcus bending over him, an anxious look on his face.

'Come on, Tom, we can't stay here. We've got to get moving.'

'Where are we?' muttered Tom. He yawned and stretched and looked around in confusion.

He was lying at the back of a pile of sacks that seemed to be filled with some sort of grain. The sacks were very dusty and there was a strange, musty smell about them. Tom was disorientated and he struggled to focus his eyes properly. He guessed that he was in some sort of store or warehouse but nothing seemed to make sense to him.

'Come on, Tom! We've got to get moving before we're discovered!'

It was noisy, too. People were shouting and someone was singing and there was a general bustle of activity.

Tom pushed himself up into a sitting position and asked the question again. 'Where are we, Marcus? What's going on?'

Marcus crouched down suddenly and raised a warning hand to Tom. 'Keep quiet,' he whispered. 'They're back!'

There was the sound of heavy footsteps on cobbles followed by a deep, gruff voice that barked out an order.

'Git a move on, yer good-fer-nothin's! There's only an hour of daylight left! We've got to git this lot across the river yet!'

Tom could hear muttering and cursing as the workers loaded the heavy sacks onto their shoulders and trudged away over the cobbles.

'Come on,' urged Marcus. 'Now's our chance. Let's get away before we're discovered.'

The two boys scrambled over the pile of dusty sacks and glanced around nervously. They were, indeed, in a storehouse. The building was built of wood and was clearly in a poor condition. Thick oak beams supported a flimsy wooden roof that seemed to be rotten and leaking. The cobbled floor was worn and uneven and it was difficult to walk across. The whole place felt cold and damp and Tom thought that it was a totally unsuitable building in which to store grain. No wonder the sacks smelt musty. There was only one way out, an open door across the cobbles at the front of the store.

'This way,' said Marcus, his voice low and urgent. 'Take care – they could be back at any moment.'

Just as they reached the exit the gruff voice

snapped out another command.

'Yer useless, the pair of yer! We've got to rope them in yet! How am I supposed to make a living with useless dolts like you working for me!'

The two boys exchanged nervous glances and instinctively darted to either side of the doorway to hide in the shadows. The useless dolts trudged through the entrance and plodded across the cobbles leaving Tom and Marcus to slip out unnoticed.

Within seconds, they were out on the wooden quayside, scurrying away from the musty store and the grumpy taskmaster.

At a safe distance, they stopped and took in the scene around them. The quayside was teeming with people. Some were busy loading and unloading boats, scuttling in and out of the never-ending rows of warehouses; some were sitting at the water's edge, their feet dangling over the wooden platform towards the murky water below; some pushed barrows full of fruit or vegetables, shouting out their wares with little or no effect. The river itself was crowded with boats, flimsy wooden constructions, barges carrying coal or piled high with huge covered bales, and one or two larger ships that displayed proud sails. There was a steady, stiff breeze, which lifted and carried bits of hay and straw and caused the loose covers to flap on the boats and barges. Tom was aware, too, of the smell – a disgusting stench that seemed to rise from the river and invade his senses.

To his left, a short distance away a most strange looking bridge traversed the river. Tom had seen nothing like it. A series of narrow arches snaked across the dark water, above which a cluster of shops and houses were built, crammed together and several storeys high.

'What is it?' asked Tom, pointing towards the unfamiliar construction.

'It's a bridge,' said Marcus, seriously.

Tom gave him a withering glance. 'I know it's a bridge, stupid – but I don't recognise it.'

'It's old London Bridge,' said Marcus. 'It was destroyed in The Fire of London. We've obviously arrived before the start of the fire.'

'The Fire of London,' repeated Tom, slowly. He was remembering the shouts and the screams and the showers of sparks that exploded into the sky as he made his escape across the heath from Hideaway House. 'The girl in the window,' he continued. 'The buildings were burning and the air was heavy with smoke. She was trapped in the house, Marcus! We've got to get to her before Hideaway House is burned to the ground!'

'That's why we're here,' said Marcus, quietly, 'to rescue the girl and take her back to the time cavern. But firstly, we've got to find your Hideaway House and hope that Hemlock hasn't moved her. Can you get us back to Hideaway House, Tom?'

Tom looked dejected. He had no idea where to find the rambling old house. 'There was a stone wall,' he said, racking his brain for clues, 'and a wooden door set in the wall. I remember it was near some open heath land but – I'm not sure. Where do we begin, Marcus? We'll never find it!'

'We'll find it,' said Marcus, confidently. 'We'll start by getting away from the river. Let's move up into the town. It'll be dark soon and we need to find somewhere to rest for the night. Keep your eyes open for anything you might recognise that could lead us to your Hideaway House.'

Several tracks led away from the river and the quayside and the boys took one of them, dodging the barrows and the traders on their way up to the town. They soon reached the labyrinth of narrow streets that made up old London Town, the shops and houses crammed together in untidy disarray. It was turning dusk and the street traders were packing up their carts and barrows, tossing any left over or unwanted goods to the floor where they would be eaten by the rats or the stray dogs that roamed the filthy streets, or they would rot and add to the strong stench that filled the air. A fishmonger tossed a pile of fish heads and entrails into the channel that ran down the middle of the road and Tom turned away in disgust as a bony cat appeared from a doorway and attacked the feast immediately.

The boys wandered along a narrow street and Tom noticed that many of the doors still had red crosses on them, although they were faded with the passing of the months since the plague had been at its height. He couldn't help but wonder how many bodies had been carried out from behind the doors and carted away in the dead of night. He shivered at the thought.

'How do we know it's the right time?' said Tom, as they turned a corner and passed a sign that said Thames Street. 'I mean, how do we know exactly where we are in time?'

'The Time Master will have taken care of that,' replied Marcus, confidently. 'He will have guided us to the right place and the right time.'

They turned into New Fish Street, where the wooden and pitch houses seemed more crammed together than ever, their upper storeys overhanging the narrow street, turning the dusk into immediate night. They passed The Star Inn, which was already crowded with noisy drinkers, the lamps casting a pale yellow glow from the small windows. One man was slumped outside the doorway, his hat pulled over his eyes, his hands clutching an empty glass that had long since spilled its contents.

The boys hurried on and turned into Pudding Lane, which was almost as dark and narrow as New Fish Street. And there was Thomas Farynor's bakery, its painted sign proudly displayed above the shop door, the baker himself brushing out the crumbs onto the cobbled street.

Tom stopped and stared at the sign in disbelief as a group of ragged street urchins taunted the baker, causing him to swing his brush at them in anger.

'Pudding Lane,' said Tom, slowly. 'The baker's shop. It's where the fire started, Marcus. We should tell him to make sure the coals in his ovens are out properly.'

Marcus smiled knowingly. 'It would make no difference,' he said. 'You can't alter what has already happened. We're just revisiting the time, Tom.'

A young boy, no more than seven years old, darted between the baker's legs as he took another swing at a scruffy girl who pulled a face at him. The boy was into the shop in seconds and Tom watched open mouthed as he grabbed two loaves and stuffed them into his shirt. The baker chased him down the lane, waving his brush in the air.

'Quick! Now's our chance!' said Marcus, and to Tom's horror he rushed into the shop and grabbed a loaf for himself. Marcus was out within seconds and he signalled for Tom to follow him away from the shop.

'But that's stealing!' protested Tom, once they were a safe distance away. 'Surely you don't believe in taking things from other people?'

'Steal or starve?' said Marcus, shortly. It's your choice?' And he broke the loaf in two and offered half to Tom.

Tom was surprised how hungry he felt and he took the bread thankfully, pushing guilty thoughts to the back of his mind.

The last minutes of daylight were fast fading and a pale moon was rising in the clear sky. A warm

breeze was still blowing, tunnelling along the narrow streets, making mini whirlwinds of bits of rubbish and debris.

'We need to find somewhere to rest for the night,' said Marcus, chewing on the remains of the loaf. 'We can't just wander the streets, it would be too dangerous.'

'What about The Star Inn?' suggested Tom. 'We passed it before we got to the baker's.'

'Oh, fine,' said Marcus sarcastically. 'We'll go and book a room, should we? Let's make sure we get one with a television!'

'I'm not talking about a room,' snapped Tom. 'There was a yard to the side of the inn, probably where they leave the horses. There were piles of straw. It might not be that comfortable but at least we would be sheltered.'

'And we could burrow into the straw,' said Marcus, warming to the idea. 'No one would see us if we were covered with straw.'

'Let's do it,' said Tom, and they turned around and headed back along Pudding Lane towards The Star Inn.

Tom glanced guiltily into the baker's shop as they passed. Thomas Farynor was there tidying his equipment away. There was a maid, too, carrying a pail of water in one hand and a huge cloth in the other. The grumpy baker shouted at her as some of the water slopped over the top of the bucket. Tom paused for a moment and took a step towards the shop door. The baker would soon be scraping the coals and ashes from his oven. Could it be that very night that the job would not be done properly?

Reading his friend's mind, Marcus placed a guiding hand on Tom's arm and said, 'Come on, Tom. It's no use – you can't change what has already happened.'

The warm September breeze seemed to be getting stronger as the two boys made their way back to The Star Inn. The drunk with the floppy hat was still there, slumped on the cobbles. The glass had fallen from his hand and it lay in fragments on the cobbled street. The inn was packed with people, singing and shouting and celebrating the fact that they had reached the end of another working day.

It was easy to get into the yard at the side of the inn as there was a wide gate large enough to allow a horse and carriage to pass through. Tom and Marcus glanced around. The street was crowded. It was dark and although there was a clear moon, it failed to light the narrow street.

The boys darted through the entrance and crossed the wide yard to where the straw lay piled high in the corner. They stooped low and looked around the untidy yard. It was cluttered; piled high with empty barrels, broken chairs and tables, an old wooden cart. Bits of straw blew everywhere, whipped up by the ever-present gusting wind. A small, rectangular window emitted a feeble yellow glow onto a section of the yard but, other than that, it was quite dark. There was a wooden door next to the window and the boys could see that it was another way into the crowded bar.

'What do we do now?' whispered Tom. He wasn't sure why he was whispering because there was no one else in the yard to hear him.

'I guess we settle down in the straw for the night,' replied Marcus, 'and then tomorrow, in the daylight, we look for your Hideaway House.'

Tom stared down at the pile of dirty straw. All of a sudden his bed did not seem so appealing. It looked a strange, yellowish-green colour and it smelt of horses.

'Come on,' said Marcus, taking the initiative and kneeling down on the straw. 'It's not that bad! It's only early evening. A lot of hours have to pass until the first light of dawn.'

Chapter 9

Fire in the Night

It was a combination of things that woke up Tom and Marcus later that night. Firstly, there was the wind that had picked up even more strength and seemed to be gusting around the inn yard. How could that be? The inn and the surrounding buildings sheltered the yard and yet the wind howled as it had done on the night of the storm when Tom was in his bedroom. Secondly, there were the frantic shouts of *Fire! Fire!* and the ensuing commotion that seemed to grow by the minute. But thirdly, and of more immediacy to the boys, was the sound of the rear door to the inn splintering into pieces as two great hulks burst through it and tumbled into the yard kicking and flailing at each other.

The men were clearly drunk and the fight was vicious. Tom and Marcus leapt up in fear and cowered back against the yard wall, hidden in the shadows. They couldn't see a great deal at first but they could certainly hear the shouting and cursing as the men laid into each other. Gradually, as their eyes grew accustomed to the darkness, Tom and Marcus picked out the great burly figures tumbling and rolling about the yard. One seemed to gain advantage for a moment and he lashed out with his foot, sending his adversary crashing into the pile of empty barrels. But the floored man was not beaten. He lifted a barrel above his head and hurled it at his enemy, who crashed to the floor with a scream of pain. The next moment they were together again, wrestling with each other like two great wounded bears. A fist flashed and there was a sickening crack. One of the men reeled backwards and landed on his back in the straw, immediately in front of the two terrified boys. The other man picked up a broken chair and advanced, slowly, a thin smile spreading across his bloodied face. It was then that Tom's blood ran cold and a shiver of terror rooted him to the spot. As the brute approached, there was no mistaking the black eye patch and the deep, purple scar that ran across his forehead. Tom had seen him before in the grounds of Hideaway House, shouting out his warning as Tom turned and ran out of the gate and over the heath.

The man on the straw rolled over, pushed himself up into a kneeling position and shook his head a few times in an attempt to help him regain his senses. He looked up to see Eye Patch towering over him, the broken chair raised above his head. Tom and Marcus looked on in horror as Eye Patch brought the chair crashing down onto his opponent. Amidst a splintering of wood, there was a gasp and a groan, the man collapsed back onto the straw and lay absolutely motionless, his head turned towards the two watching boys, his eyes open and staring.

Eye Patch stood over him for a few moments

and then took an unsteady step backwards. A sudden shower of sparks lit the night sky and turned the great man's scarred face devil-red. At the same time, Tom jerked with shock, causing Eye Patch to grunt with anger when he realised he was not alone. He focused his one good eye on the two frightened boys and, for a moment, Tom thought he was going to charge. The three of them stood absolutely still, staring at each other until a second shower of sparks seemed to stir the great man into action. He raised a hand and pointed directly at Tom and then he backed away slowly across the yard before turning unsteadily and disappearing back into the inn through the splintered doorway.

Tom sank to his knees and Marcus crouched down at his side.

'It was him,' said Tom, his voice trembling with fear. 'It was definitely him.'

'What are you talking about?' said Marcus, confused. 'Have you seen him before?'

'He was at Hideaway House,' explained Tom. 'It was as if he was there to keep guard over the girl.'

'Then he's there on Hemlock's orders,' said Marcus, his face set in a worried frown. 'We must be very careful, Tom.'

Beyond the inn walls the sky was glowing smoky red as more confused shouts split the silence. Someone was ringing a handbell as if to warn that disaster was about to strike.

'It's begun,' said Marcus, looking to the sky.

'We've got to get away from here, Tom, before the fire gets a hold.'

A patch of straw to their right was already smouldering, ignited by the last explosion of sparks.

'We need to follow him,' said Tom, suddenly appreciating the opportunity that had presented itself. 'If we follow Eye Patch he'll lead us straight to Hideaway House.'

'You're right,' agreed Marcus. 'Let's get around to the front of the inn before we lose him.'

The smouldering patch of straw burst into life and the flames snaked across the yard, setting alight the pile the boys had used as their beds. Tom and Marcus made their move. Leaving the fiery yard behind them, they passed through the gateway and stood once again in the narrow street, the strong breeze blowing straight into their faces, the commotion and shouting growing by the minute. Panic was beginning to get a grip as frightened people spilled into the streets.

'There he is!' said Tom, pointing beyond the entrance to The Star Inn. 'He must be on his way back to the house!'

Sure enough, Eye Patch was staggering over the cobbles, swaying from side to side, his huge form silhouetted against the glowing red sky.

'Let's get after him,' said Marcus. 'Keep a safe distance. We mustn't let him realise he's being followed.'

Behind them, the yard of The Star Inn was

ablaze. The broken chairs, the tables and the empty barrels had caught fire and the flames were leaping above the walls. Tom glanced behind to see the desperate innkeeper throw a bucket of water into the furnace before racing back into the building for a refill. Tom thought about the injured man lying on the cobbled yard but before he could say anything he felt Marcus's grip on his arm, pulling him forward.

'Leave it,' said Marcus, as if he could read Tom's mind. 'There's nothing we can do to help. Let's get after him.'

Eye Patch left New Fish Street and turned into a dark alleyway that seemed to run in between two streets. The two boys waited a few moments and then followed him into the alley. It was only a short passageway, so narrow that they had to walk in single file, stepping over the piles of stinking rubbish that had been left to rot. And then they were out into another street, the great man staggering ahead of them. The whole town seemed to be awake. People were standing in doorways or leaning out of upstairs windows, staring in fear towards the red glow that seemed to be spreading across the London sky.

'Where's it coming from?' shouted one man, appearing from a shop doorway in his dirty underwear.

'I dunno,' retorted another. 'I think it's The Star Inn gone up in flames.'

Tom wondered, for a moment, whether he

should stop and put them right but he thought better of the idea.

Eye Patch staggered on relentlessly, ignoring everyone and everything that was going on around him. He was moving away from the heart of the fire and the shouts of panic were becoming more distant. Eventually, he turned into a wider street and, although it was dark, Tom knew that they were not far from Hideaway House.

'We're nearly there,' he said to Marcus. 'I know we're nearly there.'

Sure enough, there was the great wall with the wooden door. Eye Patch stopped for a moment and rested one hand on the wall, he glanced around suspiciously and then lifted the latch and disappeared through the doorway into the grounds of Hideaway House, closing the door firmly behind him.

'What do we do now?' whispered Tom. 'Do we follow him in?'

'Give him a few minutes,' replied Marcus, stopping short of the doorway. 'We may as well let him get to the house.'

Dawn was beginning to break. The sky was gradually lightening but huge palls of black smoke spiralled upwards from the burning town as the fire continued to rage in the distance. Tom couldn't understand why the fire was not advancing towards Hideaway House – it was much closer the last time he had stood within the grounds – and then he realised that the wind was blowing the

wrong way. At some stage the wind would change direction and the flames would be fanned towards the house and the heath.

'Come on,' said Marcus, moving towards the wooden door. 'He's had long enough.'

Marcus lifted the latch and opened the door slowly. He stepped through and looked around cautiously, signalling for Tom to follow. There was no sign of Eye Patch. He had obviously gone straight into the house, leaving the two boys free to plan their next move. The boys started along the narrow path, overgrown with weeds and brambles, that led down to the driveway. Once on the drive, they could make out the shape of the great house, dark and sombre against the early morning sky.

'She was in the top window,' said Tom, indicating where he had seen the girl. 'She looked straight down at me and hammered on the window for help. It was then that Eye Patch appeared from around the side of the house. I was so scared I ran away, Marcus. I ran away and left her. Was that an awful thing to do? I should have tried to help her, shouldn't I?'

'It was the right thing to do,' said Marcus, quietly, 'and we're both going to help her now. We're going to get her out of there and take her back to the time forest.'

'But how do we know she's still there?' questioned Tom. 'There's no lamp lit in the room this time.'

'She's there,' said Marcus, confidently. 'Let's

get closer and see if we can find a way into the house without being noticed.'

The boys kept to the edge of the driveway so that they could dart into the bushes if Eye Patch reappeared but there was no sign of any movement as they approached the dark building. At the end of the driveway, three stone slabs formed steps up to the main entrance. However, it was clear that the solid wooden door had not been used for some time. It was covered with cobwebs and the hinges appeared to be locked solid with rust. Marcus tried to lift the iron latch but it would not budge.

'It's no use,' he said, 'let's move around the side. Eye Patch must have used another entrance.'

Tom peered in through a window but the glass was dirty and the room inside was so dark that he couldn't make out a thing. Slowly, they edged around the building, picking their way through the weeds and brambles that were doing their best to reclaim the building.

And then they found it - a small wooden door that Tom guessed had once led into the kitchen area or the servants quarters. It had clearly been opened recently for the brambles had been pulled to one side and the weeds flattened and trodden down. The door itself was slightly ajar and the boys stood and stared at it, neither one wanting to make the next move.

'How do we know he's not waiting for us on the other side of the door?' asked Tom, his heart pounding again with fear.

Marcus thought for a moment and then replied, 'He wouldn't know anyone was following him, Tom. He was in such a state that he's probably collapsed into sleep by now.'

'I guess you're right,' said Tom, and he edged forward and pushed the door ever so slowly. It swung inwards to reveal a small, rectangular room, dark and totally empty. 'It's clear,' confirmed Tom. 'Let's go in.'

They stepped down into the room and glanced around quickly. It was lined with wooden shelves but they were completely empty. Tom was breathing heavily and he was sure that he could hear his own heart pounding.

'This way,' said Marcus, indicating another door in the far wall. The second room led into a larger area that had clearly been used as a kitchen. The surfaces were dusty and cobwebs hung down in clusters from the low ceiling. They crept through the room into a large hallway. Growing in confidence, they stood in the hallway and looked upwards. The whole house seemed to be covered in dust and cobwebs but it was obvious that someone was using the building as the dust had been disturbed and large footprints were clearly visible.

A wide stairway led to the upper floor and the two boys looked towards it and then nodded at each other. Marcus took the lead, climbing slowly but steadily, stopping every so often to listen for any sign of danger. They reached the top of the stairway without incident. They had a choice. To their left, a small passageway led to two doors, both of them open so that the boys could see into the empty rooms. To their right, a wider passage led to three rooms, all of them closed.

Tom was beginning to feel uneasy again and he wasn't sure why. 'If she's here at all she'll be behind one of the closed doors,' he whispered, and Marcus nodded in agreement.

Tom moved forward to the first door and placed his hand on the latch. He took a deep breath, lifted the latch and pushed the door inwards. Nothing. The room was completely empty. It hadn't been used for some time.

'Try the next one,' whispered Marcus, and he followed Tom along the passageway.

Again Tom lifted the latch and pushed against the door. This time the hinges were stiffer and the old door creaked as it gave way to the pressure. The result was the same – the room was empty.

Tom moved to the third door and stared at it. He was breathing heavily and his hands trembled. He looked to the floor and noticed that the dust had been disturbed.

'Go on, open it!' urged Marcus.

Tom reached forward and released the latch. The door swung inwards at once and Tom let out a gasp of shock. Silhouetted against the window was a young girl, her eyes wide with terror, her hands raised to her mouth. She didn't speak, she just stood there and stared at the two boys and Tom and Marcus stared back at her.

Tom stepped into the room and Marcus followed him, neither of them able to utter a sound. They took a few hesitant paces forward but the frightened girl seemed to be looking beyond them.

Suddenly, the door slammed shut and the boys jumped with fear. Tom was the first to turn and there was Eye Patch in front of him, his fists clenched, his one good eye staring wide, his fearsome form filling the doorway and blocking any possible route of escape.

Chapter 10

Trapped

Nobody spoke for a moment and then Eye Patch's lips creased into a thin, cruel smile.

'D'you think I'm stupid?' he barked. He wiped a streak of saliva from his chin with the back of his hand. 'D'you think I didn't know you were followin' me?'

Neither of the two boys spoke and the girl remained over by the window, trembling with fear.

Eye Patch took a step forward and laughed out loud.

'I knew y' were there all the time – since I left The Star Inn. I knew you was both followin' me! I just played y' along! I'm too smart for y', aint I?'

'I – I guess so,' stammered Tom. He had never felt so frightened in his life.

'You're not as smart as you think,' snapped Marcus, defiantly. 'After all, you've led us to Hideaway House, haven't you?'

Eye Patch stiffened with rage. His mouth quivered and another dribble of saliva escaped. His one good eye seemed to turn blood red.

'You don't answer back!' he bellowed, taking another step forward. 'You don't answer back until I tell yer to, see? You try and be smart with me and I'll give y' the back of me hand!'

The young girl started sobbing quietly as

Marcus stood his ground and stared in defiance. 'What are you going to do with us?' he asked. 'You can't keep us here.'

'Don't you tell me what I can't do!' stormed the big man. 'That's exactly what I'm going to do – keep you here until The Master decides about you – then I'll be back to deal with you, if the fire doesn't get y' first!'

Tom felt a surge of panic. 'But you can't leave us here! Hideaway House will be destroyed!'

'What do I care!' snapped Eye Patch, sneering at the frightened boy. 'What do I care about anything!'

He wiped the saliva from his chin and backed out of the room. There was a sharp click as a key turned in the lock and then silence, apart from the steady sobbing of the young girl.

Tom and Marcus didn't move. They stood in the bare room and stared at the closed door and then, after a few moments, they exchanged worried glances.

'Not quite what I had planned,' said Marcus, and he turned to face the girl. 'Don't worry,' he said, more gently. 'It's going to be all right. We've come to get you out of here.'

The girl wiped the tears from her eyes and said in a quivering voice, 'I've been waiting for you. I thought you were never going to come.'

'I don't understand,' said Tom. 'I know you were trying to contact me. Why did you try to reach me for help?'

The girl glanced nervously towards Marcus and before she could reply he said, 'All that will become clear, Tom – but let's leave it until later. We need to concentrate on getting out of here.'

'Well at least you can tell me your name,' said Tom, annoyed that the girl had not been allowed to answer for herself.

'I'm Alice,' replied the girl, looking surprised. 'I thought you would have known that, Tom.'

'Why is he keeping you here?' continued Tom. 'Why is Eye Patch keeping you prisoner?'

'It's not Eye Patch we need to worry about,' said Marcus, 'it's Hemlock. All this is Hemlock's work and we need to escape from here and get back to the time forest or everything will be lost.'

For the first time, Tom looked around the room. There was not a lot to see. A small window gave a view back towards the gate in the wall and beyond to London Town. A pile of old, ragged blankets lay heaped in one corner of the room on the bare, uneven floorboards. Alice had placed a wooden chair next to the window so that she could sit and watch the days pass by, other than that, the room was empty. Tom couldn't imagine spending day after day in such a barren environment.

Tom looked again at Alice. There seemed to be something familiar about her face, her eyes, even the tone of her voice. It was almost as if he had met her before somewhere – but he couldn't have; surely he couldn't? The only times he had seen her she had been a ghostly white figure or a distant face in a small window. He was about to question her again when Marcus spoke.

'We need to get away from here before we travel back to the forest. I can feel Hemlock's presence. He has power over this place.'

'Great,' said Tom, looking around the empty room and staring towards the locked door. 'Have you any suggestions, Marcus?'

Marcus moved across to the window, his eyes searching for any possible escape route.

'That's no good,' he said, more to himself than to anyone else. 'Even if we smashed the window there's no way down to the ground. It's too far to jump, that's for sure.'

'What if he comes back?' said Alice. 'We can't just wait for him to deal with us!'

'There must be an answer,' said Marcus, and he sat down on the wooden chair and rested his head in his hands.

Tom stared at him for a moment and then his eyes widened with inspiration.

'That's it!' he announced. 'I think I've got it, Marcus! I think I've found the answer – or rather you have!'

Alice and Marcus exchanged confused glances.

'Perhaps you'd like to share it with us?' suggested Marcus.

'Actually, you're sitting on it!' said Tom, and he pointed at the old, wooden chair.

'It's a chair,' said Marcus. 'I'm sitting on a chair. How is an old, wooden chair going to get us out of here?'

'No, it's not a chair,' said Tom, 'it's a weapon. Do you remember the last time we saw a chair, Marcus? It was being used as a weapon. Eye Patch brought it crashing down on that poor man's head!'

Alice looked confused but Marcus was beginning to understand. He stood up and stared at the old, wooden chair.

'We'd have to get it absolutely right,' he said. 'Timing would be important.'

'We can do it,' said Tom. 'It's our only chance, Marcus. We've got to give it a try.'

Time seemed to pass so slowly. The two boys had worked out their plan, going over and over every last detail so that each knew exactly what the other was doing. Alice was involved, too. She would have an important part to play. However, they couldn't put the plan into action until Eye Patch returned – and time seemed to pass so slowly.

Tom kept returning to the window and looking back towards the town. As he stared into the smoky distance, his thoughts turned to his home and to his family. In his mind he could picture his house and his cosy bedroom. He could see himself curled up on the couch watching television, or snuggled down beneath the covers of his lovely warm bed. Even his sister Serena didn't seem so bad. She couldn't help being spotty and spiteful. What if something went wrong and he didn't return home? What if his friends Beefy and Chris were waiting for him at the street corner ready to walk to school and he never turned up? Suppose Eye Patch returned and carried out his threat to deal with them? It was too terrible to contemplate. Tom shook his head and looked again towards the distant town. The morning sky was blackened by an ever-spreading cloud of smoke, beneath which the flames leapt and the sparks exploded. By mid day the wind had changed direction. It seemed to be blowing harder than ever, gusting towards the open heathland and venting its anger on Hideaway House. At the same time, the fire was spreading upwards from the town, engulfing everything that stood in its path. It would not be long before it reached the outer wall and then engulfed the house itself.

'What if he doesn't come back for us?' said Tom. He was beginning to doubt that his plan would work. 'What if Eye Patch leaves us here to die in the fire?'

'Hemlock wouldn't allow that to happen,' replied Marcus, confidently. 'He needs Alice and he needs you, Tom. You're part of the secret too, Tom. He can't afford to lose you.'

'The bushes are alight!' said Alice, her voice trembling with fear again. 'The fire has got into the grounds and the bushes are burning!'

The three children stared out of the small window to see the flames spreading across the ground, destroying everything in their relentless drive towards Hideaway House. But Tom stared through the flames towards the pathway that led up to the small, wooden gate in the wall. It was shrouded in smoke but he could still make out the figure on the path, staring up at the window, just as he had done himself the first time he had visited Hideaway House. Was it Hemlock himself who had come to take control of the situation? Tom shivered as his blood ran cold with the thought. Yet there was something familiar about the figure. Even though it was so far away there was something familiar about the way it stood, statue still and stared up towards the watchers in the window.

Tom found his voice. 'Look!' he said, pointing towards the pathway. 'There's someone there, Marcus! On the path over by the gate!'

Marcus strained his eyes to see but the smoke had closed in again and by the time it had cleared the figure had gone.

'Come on,' said Marcus, pulling Tom away from the window. 'We've got to get in position, he's going to come for us any time now.'

Tom grabbed hold of the wooden chair and moved across the room, positioning himself to the side of the locked door. Alice and Marcus stayed near the window ready to play their part in the escape plan.

'Are you ready?' said Tom.
'Ready!' confirmed Marcus.
Alice just nodded.

'Let's go, then!' said Tom.

Alice and Marcus immediately let out a torrent of screams. They yelled and screamed and stamped and jumped up and down on the bare boards. Tom joined in, banging with his fists on the locked door. The noise rose to a deafening crescendo, so loud that Tom had to react like lightning when the key clicked in the lock and the latch jerked upwards. His heart was pounding but he knew what had to be done. Tom leapt back and raised the chair above his head in readiness. As the door flew open, Tom had a vision of Eye Patch standing over his victim in the yard of The Star Inn. This time Eye Patch himself was the victim. The big man took two strides into the room before Tom brought the chair crashing down across the back of his head and shoulders. As the chair splintered into pieces, Eye Patch let out a yell of pain. He staggered forward towards Marcus and Alice, one arm outstretched, his good eye bloodshot and staring, and then he crashed to the floor where he lay sprawled in a contorted heap.

Tom stood above him clutching what was left of the splintered chair. He was shaking from fear at what he had just done.

'Come on!' urged Marcus. 'He won't be down for long!'

Eye Patch was already regaining his senses. He was groaning and struggling to push himself up into a kneeling position. Marcus grabbed hold of Alice's hand and the three prisoners dashed for the door. And then they were out in the passageway and the stairs were in sight.

'You go first!' yelled Tom. 'I'll be right behind you!'

Alice and Marcus raced for the stairs as Tom turned to take one last look into the bare room. It was then that he saw the key. It must have fallen from Eye Patch's grasp as he burst into the room and it was lying on the floor just outside the doorway. Tom dashed back and picked it up. He could see Eye Patch staggering to his feet. Tom pulled the door closed and rammed the key into the lock. It wouldn't turn! The key wouldn't turn! Eye Patch was on his feet and the key wouldn't turn!

'Leave it!' yelled Marcus from the top of the stairs. 'Get away from the door, Tom!'

Tom gave one last desperate try and the lock suddenly clicked into place. There was a mighty roar from inside the room and the solid door shuddered as Eye Patch flung his full weight against it.

'Come on!' yelled Marcus, and they leapt down the stairs, leaving the great man to vent his anger on the locked door.

The front of the house was already ablaze. Smoke was billowing along the hallway and a snake of flame had reached the bottom of the stairs. The dry timbers were crackling and snapping in the fierce heat and the fire was spreading with frightening speed.

'Let's get out the way we entered,' yelled

Marcus. 'Through the kitchen to the side entrance.'

They were out of the house within minutes but they were not clear of danger. The dry brambles and bushes were engulfed in flames and, as the children raced around the side of the building and along the narrow path, it was clear that the house itself was turning into an inferno.

They crossed the scorched earth and reached the door in the wall charred and blackened from the heat of the relentless fire. Tom didn't try to open it, he just kicked the remnants of wood away so that they could pass through onto the heath.

The children turned to take one last look at Hideaway House. Flames had burst through the roof and a pillar of black smoke was spiralling into the heavy sky. And then Tom saw the window, the same window behind which they had been prisoners just a few minutes earlier. His blood froze as he saw a fearsome silhouette against a background of fiery red flames. Eye Patch was still in there. Even with his strength, he had been unable to break down the solid wooden door and he was still in there! He was trapped in the bare room and the house was burning around him! There was a sudden roar as the roof collapsed and an explosion of flame blew out the window. Tom gasped and took a few steps forward towards the house but Marcus grabbed him by the arm and pulled him back.

'Leave it, Tom. There's nothing we can do.'

The three children stepped through the

charred gate out onto the heath and turned their backs on the final destructive moments of Hideaway House.

Chapter 11

The Boat on the River

The heath was already swarming with people trying to escape from the blazing town. There were people pushing carts loaded with the few possessions they had been able to save; there were people carrying sacks and boxes, mothers dragging children and grown men carrying elderly relatives on their backs. The scene was chaotic and nobody seemed to know exactly where they were going.

The problem was the wind, the relentless wind that was gusting stronger than ever. The heath itself was ablaze and the flames were spreading rapidly across the dry scrubland.

'I don't understand it! It's changed direction again!' yelled one man, his young daughter perched sobbing on his shoulders. 'Down to the river! We're better taking the track down to the river!'

Those near enough to hear his words of advice followed him while others continued to struggle across the blackened heath, the scorched ground burning beneath their feet.

'What shall we do?' shouted Tom, looking around in desperation. 'Which is the best way to go?'

'Follow him down to the river,' replied Marcus. 'He seems to know what he's doing.'

The track to the river was not easy; it was overgrown and uneven. People were pushing and shoving each other in their haste to escape the spreading fire. Alice, weak from her ordeal, stumbled more than once and Marcus did his best to support and encourage her.

'Come on,' he urged, 'we've got this far we're not about to give in now!'

They were soon back on the quayside, further down river than when they had first arrived, nearer to London Bridge. If anything, the scene was even more chaotic. There were shouts and screams and yells of despair. The bridge itself was ablaze and the river, crowded with boats, was also littered with debris and various items that people had tried to salvage from their burning shops and houses.

Suddenly, a terrific explosion ripped through the air as one of the storehouses blew up. Pieces of burning timber rained down from the sky as panic spread and the screams reached a new crescendo.

Tom, Marcus and Alice joined in the panic and ran for all they were worth along the crowded quayside, hampered by the hoards of people desperately searching for a means of escape. Tom barged into a fat man carrying a sack of vegetables, causing him to lose his grip so that carrots and potatoes spilled across the quayside. The man cursed and swore and as he bent down to retrieve his goods somebody else fell over him. And then Alice stumbled again. She pitched forward and lay sprawled on the damp wooden boards. Marcus knelt down to try and help her up as a man to his right untied the rope to a small boat.

'It's three kids, John! They're on their own!'

The voice belonged to his wife, who was already seated in the boat, clasping a young baby as close to her as she possibly could.

'Get them on board! We can't leave them to fend for themselves!'

John hesitated for a moment, anxious not to waste time in getting his own family to safety.

'Get them on board!' repeated his wife. 'We're not moving 'til you get them on the boat!'

'Come on,' said John, extending a hand to Alice, 'we've no time to lose.'

The boat was tiny. There was a narrow plank of wood at one end, upon which John's wife was sitting, clutching the baby close to her chest. A wider plank crossed the middle of the boat, clearly meant for the person who took the oars. There was a small space at the other end of the boat that was barely big enough for one person, let alone three. It was into this space that Tom, Marcus and Alice squeezed, Marcus perching precariously on the very rim of the boat. Alice, her knees grazed and bleeding, was crying quietly.

'Hold on,' said John, gripping a paddle in each hand. 'We're heading down river.'

The boat pulled away from the burning quayside ever so slowly. It seemed low in the water, clearly overloaded with too many people.

John pulled for all he was worth and the boat eased out into the dark, crowded river.

'Thank you,' said Tom, his voice shaking with relief. 'Thank you for helping us.'

'It's all right, my love,' replied John's wife. 'We've all got to help each other at times like this. Where's the rest of your family?'

Before anyone could answer, a savage gust of wind tossed the tiny boat from side to side causing Marcus to gasp with shock and tighten his grip.

'I don't understand it,' he said, more to himself than to anyone in particular. 'The wind – it's almost as if ...'

He left the sentence unfinished.

Tom noticed that Alice was shivering and he placed an arm around her shoulder. 'Are you all right?' he asked.

'I think so,' she said, forcing a weak smile. 'I'm just glad to be away from that place.' She paused for a moment and then she stared straight into Tom's eyes and said, 'You came for me, Tom. I knew you wouldn't let me down.'

Another gust of wind almost caused Marcus to lose his balance. John cursed as he struggled to keep the boat on course.

'Where are we heading for?' asked Tom, and he glanced over towards the quayside to see how far out they had travelled.

It was then that his blood ran cold. A crumbling wooden jetty jutted out over the river from the burning embankment. John would have to pull further out into the river to avoid hitting it. But it was not the smouldering obstruction that put fear into Tom's heart, it was the terrifying figure that stood astride the jetty, waiting to pounce as the boat passed.

'No ...' said Tom, his voice trembling with apprehension. 'No... no... it can't be!'

Marcus swivelled round as the boat got ever closer to the jetty. At the same time, Alice raised her hands to her face and let out a scream. There was Eye Patch, balanced at the very end of the jetty, his clothes hanging from him in burnt tatters, his hair singed, his face blistered and blackened.

'What's the matter?' yelled John's wife, as the small boat got nearer and nearer to the jetty. 'What is it that's frightening you?'

'Pull further out into the river!' yelled Tom, in desperation. 'We're going to hit the jetty!'

'I can't!' shouted John, straining to keep control. 'The boat's not responding... Maybe it's the wind ... I can't pull any harder!'

The wind gusted again and the smouldering jetty loomed ever closer. And then Tom's attention was caught by something beyond the jetty. Another boat was drifting in, a much larger boat that seemed completely out of control. It, too, was caught by the driving wind and the two boats were on a collision course.

'Look out!' yelled Tom – but it was too late.

There was an almighty crack and a jolt as the

larger vessel rammed into the side of John's flimsy boat sending it reeling towards the wooden jetty. Eye Patch let out a blood curdling yell and at the same time, Marcus lost his balance completely and tumbled into the filthy river. The boat smashed into the edge of the jetty, catapulting Eye Patch off the end and into the swirling water. John's wife screamed and Alice clung hold even tighter to Tom, her fingernails digging into his arm.

'Marcus!' yelled Tom, and turning to John he shouted, 'He's gone overboard! We've got to help him!'

John looked pale and shaken. He had been thrown forward and he had let go of the paddles, one falling to the bottom of the boat while the other had disappeared over the side. Dazed and confused, he edged forward to comfort his sobbing wife, who was still clutching tight hold of her screaming child. The other boat had veered away into the middle of the river, it's frightened passengers confused and shaken.

The whole jetty had collapsed with the force of the blow – but Marcus was all right. He had struck out for the quayside and was standing waist deep near the edge of the water. It was Eye Patch who was in trouble. He was thrashing around in the dirty water, reaching out in desperation at pieces of the broken jetty, shouting out for someone to help him. He couldn't swim and he was floundering, fighting for his life in the grasping river.

Tom and Alice stared in horror as Eye Patch disappeared beneath the surface and then reappeared, thrashing and grabbing at the bits and pieces that floated past.

'Help me!' he screamed. 'For God's sake, help me!'

Tom instinctively grabbed the paddle from the bottom of the boat and plunged it into the dark water, pulling for all he was worth, first on one side and then on the other side of the small boat, edging closer and closer to the drowning man. Eye Patch disappeared again and then resurfaced yards from the boat, coughing and spluttering and choking on the dirty water. Alice buried her head in her hands as Eye Patch's burnt and blistered face loomed towards her. Tom gave a final pull so that he was alongside the big man and then he reached out the paddle towards him.

'Grab hold!' he yelled. 'Take hold of the paddle!'

Eye Patch lunged forward and grabbed the end of the paddle, almost pulling Tom out of the boat with the force of his grip. John moved forward to help and, together, he and Tom hauled the big man forward so that his arms were over the edge of the boat.

Alice couldn't look at him. Most of his straggly hair had been singed and burnt from his head and his black eye patch had come off in the water to reveal the closed socket that had been roughly stitched together.

John took the paddle and slowly hauled the small boat towards the quayside, where Marcus waited to help drag it in. He was soaking wet and shivering. Eye Patch clung on for dear life until the water was shallow enough for him to drag himself to his feet. He stood knee deep in the water for a moment, tottering unsteadily, his breath still coming in gasps, and then a cruel grin spread slowly across his blackened face.

'You fools!' he spluttered. 'Fancy helping Eye Patch when you could have escaped! You stupid fools!'

He lunged forward in the water and made a grab towards Alice who, too terrified to move, let out a piercing scream. Tom didn't hesitate. He grabbed the paddle from John and swung it with all his force so that it smacked against the side of the great man's head. Eye Patch stopped stone still in the murky water. His mouth dropped open and his one good eye stared wide in disbelief, and then slowly, ever so slowly, he toppled backwards and floated motionlessly in the dirty water. Tom prodded the paddle into his limp body, pushing it so that it floated and then wedged in the thick mud at the side of the river. He glared up at Marcus, who was staring in astonished admiration.

'That's the second time I've laid him out today,' said Tom, and he sank back into the boat, completely exhausted.

The three children nestled down on the makeshift

bed of straw they had laid for themselves. After disposing of Eye Patch they had walked for hours along the crowded riverbank with John and his family, away from the spreading fire and the smouldering heath. Despite the warm breeze, Marcus was freezing cold, shivering from his tumble in the river. Tom was worried about him. He was so cold that his teeth were actually chattering.

'My brother will sort you out,' John had assured him, putting a comforting arm around the boy's shoulder. 'We'll get you out of these sodden clothes and my brother will find you some fresh ones. They may be a bit big for you but they'll serve the purpose.'

Eventually, they had reached the small stone building that John referred to as his brother's cottage. It didn't look like a cottage to Tom. Tom had stayed in a cottage when he had been on holiday to Cornwall. This just consisted of two rooms and an outbuilding that had been used for housing pigs. Luckily, the pigs had been taken to market the previous week and, although the building still smelt awful, it was warm and there was a pile of fresh straw in one corner.

Tom didn't care where he was as long as he could rest. He was so exhausted that he would have slept with the pigs had he been required to do so.

'What do we do now?' he asked, shifting in the straw so that it moulded roughly to the shape of his body.

Surprisingly, it was Alice who answered.

'We travel back to the time forest,' she said, sitting cross-legged at Tom's side. 'We must get away from here before Hemlock comes after us again. Now that we're not in his presence we'll be able to make our journey.'

'You know about the time forest?' said Tom. 'And Hemlock – I don't understand?'

'Of course I know about the time forest,' replied Alice. 'It was from the time forest that I was snatched. And yes – I know all about Hemlock and I know about you, Tom.'

'How do you know about me?' said Tom, with more than a hint of suspicion. 'Who exactly are you? What is this secret you're supposed to have?'

'All in good time,' interrupted Marcus. 'Save your questions until we're safely back with The Time Master, Tom. We need to rest. We have a long journey ahead of us.'

Tom did not have the strength to argue. He was so exhausted that he was finding it difficult to talk. His head was full of images; the vicious fight in the cobbled yard of The Star Inn, Alice cowering in fear by the window in the bare room; Hideaway House collapsing in a confusion of flames; crowds of desperate people carrying boxes and bundles of clothes, wading into the dirty river; Eye Patch tottering on the scorched jetty, waiting to pounce on the feeble wooden boat. The images merged and swirled around Tom's mind as he drifted into an uneasy sleep. And then Marcus and Alice were there with him in his unconscious world. They were all holding hands and they were falling, spinning around in the darkness, falling, falling, falling endlessly through time…

Chapter 12

Journey's End

Tom opened his eyes to see a ring of faces staring down at him. For a moment he thought he was still in his dream but when one of the faces spoke he realised that he was conscious, even though he didn't have a clue where he was.

'Are you all right, Tom? We've been worried about you.'

Tom slowly turned his head towards the voice and his eyes gradually focused on Rosie's face. Tom didn't answer. He lay there for a few moments in the orange glow cast by the flickering lamps in the time cavern. He moved his eyes around the circle, pausing on each face until he remembered the name. There was Marcus – and Alice – and ….. who was that? Oh, yes, of course – it was The Time Master. Tom looked anxiously for another face. Someone was missing. Where was Carlos? Tom closed his eyes and he was back there, staring out of the window from the bare room in Hideaway House. There was someone on the path, watching and waiting. Tom thought he recognised the figure – but it couldn't be …

Tom reopened his eyes and suddenly sat bolt upright. 'Where's Carlos?' he demanded. 'Why isn't he here?'

'It's all right, Tom. He is here,' said The Time

Master, softly.

The circle of faces moved back and parted to reveal Carlos, standing in the background with his arms folded, his face completely expressionless.

'Welcome back,' said Carlos. 'Marcus has told us all about your journey. You should be proud of yourself.'

'You should be very proud,' agreed The Time Master. 'You've saved your sister from the clutches of Hemlock.'

Tom's eyes widened with disbelief. 'My sister!' He stared at Alice, who smiled back at him, gently. 'Did you say – my sister?'

'That's right, Tom,' confirmed The Time Master. 'Alice is your twin sister. Surely you can see the similarities? She looks just like you.'

Tom couldn't speak for a few moments. He sat there with his mouth open, staring from one face to another. Eventually, his gaze settled on Alice and it was as if his own hazel green eyes were staring back at him. He turned back to The Time Master and said, 'What about Serena? She's my sister, isn't she?'

'Come over here,' said The Time Master, taking hold of Tom's arm. 'There are a few things I need to explain to you.'

The Time Master led Tom over to the stone slab in the small chamber, the others followed and sat on the floor in front of them.

'You know that you are adopted, don't you, Tom? You know that Mr and Mrs Travis are not your real mother and father?'

'I know that,' said Tom, defensively. 'And Serena's not my real sister. It's never been a secret. I know they're not my real family.'

'And you know that you were found in Greenwich, abandoned as a baby?'

'Yes, I know that, too,' said Tom. 'I was left in a cardboard box outside the gates of The Royal Observatory. I was discovered by an old tramp called Thomas. That's where I got my name from. Serena keeps reminding me that I'm named after an old tramp!'

The Time Master looked serious. 'What you don't know, Tom, is that you were not alone when you were discovered. Alice was there with you, by your side in the cardboard box. Your real parents had left you there because they knew you were in danger. Your mother had placed a letter in the box with you but the old tramp couldn't read. When he saw the letter he just screwed it up and threw it away but he had the sense to get you both to the hospital. He saved your lives, Tom. It was a freezing cold night and that old tramp saved your lives.'

'What happened to my parents?' said Tom, quietly. 'Are they dead?'

'No, they're not dead, Tom, but they are Hemlock's prisoners, just as Alice was. Hemlock took them that very same night, just a couple of hours after they had left you outside The Royal Observatory. They were powerless to resist him.

Your parents are trapped somewhere in time and it's up to us to rescue them.'

'How will we do that?' asked Tom. 'How will we rescue them if we don't know where they are?'

'They will find you, Tom. Now that you've begun travelling they will find you, just as Alice did, then we'll be able to rescue them.'

Tom thought for a few moments and then, turning to Alice, he said, 'What happened to you, Alice? Did Hemlock take you from the hospital?'

'No,' said Alice, 'we were separated and I was adopted by a different family. I grew up with them, made friends and went to school like any normal child. I didn't realise I was different until I began to experience strange dreams.' Alice smiled and glanced at Rosie. 'Everyone knows that girls are far more advanced than boys,' she continued. 'I learnt to travel well before you, Tom. I visited the time forest, as all travellers do, and I met the friends. Everything was fine until once when I arrived, Hemlock was waiting for me. It was terrible. The forest turned pitch black and there was thunder and lightning. I just ran and ran through the trees until I collapsed to the ground. I don't remember anything else until I woke up in Hideaway House.'

'You say Hemlock was waiting for you?' repeated Tom. 'So you've seen him? You know what he looks like?'

'Nobody really sees Hemlock,' interrupted

The Time Master. 'You might see shadows or you might feel his presence but you will never actually look into his eyes. Should that happen, it would probably be the last thing you would do.'

There was so much for Tom to think about. His mind was swimming and he felt as if he was drowning in a sea of revelations.

'I don't understand why Hemlock should want to destroy my family,' said Tom. 'What's so special about us?'

'Oh, he doesn't want to destroy you or your family,' explained The Time Master. 'Just the opposite, in fact. He needs to keep you all very safe. Together, you hold the secret he has been striving after - and he very nearly succeeded, Tom. He had your mother and your father and your twin sister trapped in time and he very nearly had you, Tom. If he could have got all of you together the secret would have been his. Only then would Hemlock have destroyed you. You ruined his plans, Tom – and he'll never forgive you. Hemlock will hunt you down mercilessly – but, rest assured, we will be here to help you.'

'What about Alice?' asked Tom. 'Will she stay with you in the time forest? Will you protect her as well?'

'Of course we'll protect Alice,' said The Time Master. 'She'll go back to her family and get on with her life, just as you will – but we'll always meet together in the time forest and we'll always fight against Hemlock.' The Time Master stood up and moved a few paces away from the stone slab. 'Now, it's time for you to go, Tom. Your first journey is over. We'll talk again soon.'

'No, I'm not tired!' protested Tom, but his eyes were already feeling heavy and his head was beginning to swim.

'Goodbye, Tom,' said Marcus. 'We shared a great journey together.'

'Goodbye, Tom.' Rosie's voice was soft and gentle. 'Don't wait too long to return to the forest.'

The lights in the time cavern were flickering and the friend's faces were fading.

'Goodbye, Tom,' whispered Alice, and she reached forward and brushed his fair hair away from his eyes with her hand. 'We'll be together again soon ...'

For once, Thomas Travis was not late for school. A whole week had passed since his incredible journey and Tom was feeling quite rested. However, he was about to pay the price for his punctuality.

Tom recognised the danger and he quickened his pace as he approached Melissa Morgan's house. He could see Chris and Beefy waiting for him at the end of the street, urging him to hurry past the danger zone. It was no good. Just as he reached Melissa's front gate her curtains twitched and within seconds her front door had opened and she was flouncing down the path, all white teeth and blonde curls.

'Oh, Thomas!' she crooned, in feigned

surprise. 'Fancy me coming out just as you were walking past!'

Chris and Beefy had collapsed into a heap of laughter at the end of the street.

'Fancy!' said Tom, doing his best not to scowl.

'Shall we walk to school together, Tom? That would be nice, wouldn't it?'

'Wonderful!' said Tom, and he deliberately wiped his nose on his sleeve in the hope that Melissa would be disgusted.

'Have you got a cold?' she whined, delving into her pocket. 'Here – you can have some of my tissues. My mum always sends me to school with a little packet of tissues.'

Tom stared in disbelief at the pink tissues, which had a little picture of Barbie in one corner.

'Thanks!' he said, and he snatched them from Melissa's grasp and stuffed them into his pocket as Chris and Beefy approached.

'What's that you've got?' asked Beefy, grinning annoyingly. 'Has your girlfriend given you a present, Tom?'

'Take no notice of him,' said Melissa, putting a comforting hand on Tom's arm. 'He's a great jealous lump, that's what he is!'

They crossed the road with Mrs Briggs, the lollipop lady, and walked the short distance to school. The morning was crisp and clear and the sky was blue. Tom was feeling more at ease than he had done for weeks. In his mind, he knew that there would be other journeys, more dangers to face, but he knew also that The Time Master and the friends would be there to guide him.

'You seem so much better, Tom,' said Mrs Howarth, as she gave out the literacy books after morning registration. 'It's almost as if I've got a new boy in my class!'

Tom smiled politely and opened his book in readiness to work.

'Now then,' began Mrs Howarth from the front of the class. 'Last week we watched a video all about The Great Fire of London.'

Tom stiffened and a shiver of apprehension passed through his body.

'This morning, children,' continued the teacher, 'I want you to write a story about the event. I want you to imagine you were there in September 1666 when the fire broke out. Just close your eyes for a few moments and try to picture the scene...'

'I don't think I'd better do that,' said Tom out loud.

Luckily, Mrs Howarth didn't hear him but Chris and Beefy gave him a puzzled stare.

'I want you to include plenty of description. Your stories should be descriptive and very exciting. Now, let's do a bit of planning first ...'

To his surprise, Tom was all right. There was no dizziness, no falling or spinning sensation and no faces flashing past his eyes. He put his head down and he got on with his work. Tom liked writing stories – and what a tale he would have to tell!

Later that evening, just as Tom was settling down to watch his favourite soap on television, the most awful scream rent the air. Mrs Travis leapt from her chair with her hand on her heart. The scream was followed by a prolonged wailing sound that seemed to be coming from somewhere upstairs.

'Oh, my goodness!' panted Tom's mum. 'It's our Serena! What on earth's the matter with her?'

Tom, looking completely disinterested, used the remote control to turn the volume up on the television.

'Switch that thing off!' snapped Mrs Travis. 'Your sister's in distress! Let's go and see what's wrong.'

Tom sighed and pulled himself out of the chair. Serena was always in distress. She'd probably discovered another pimple on her nose.

The moment Mrs Travis reached the top of the stairs, the smell hit her. It was an awful smell, like a rotting, dead rat and Mrs Travis clasped her hand over her mouth before entering Serena's room.

Tom hung back, guiltily.

Once the bedroom door was open, the smell was ten times worse. Serena was huddled at the top of her bed, tears were streaming down her face, which had turned a sickly shade of pale green.

'What in heaven's name is the matter?' said Mrs Travis, rushing into the room to comfort her distraught daughter.

'It's him!' wailed Serena, pointing towards her brother, who lingered in the doorway. 'It's got to be him.'

Tom was holding his nose and wafting the air.

'What do you mean?' implored Mrs Travis. 'Thomas hasn't done anything. He's been downstairs watching television with me.'

Serena indicated towards her wardrobe. A plastic bag lay split open on the floor by the open wardrobe door. Something green and slimy had seeped out and dribbled onto the carpet. As Mrs Travis stared at it, the blob seemed to be steaming.

'I needed some socks and I thought they were in the bag,' wailed Serena. 'I ripped it open and … o-oh-oh! It's disgusting! Horrible, rotten, smelly, furry fish!'

Mrs Travis's expression changed to one of anger. She turned towards the doorway but Tom had disappeared. He was already in his own room, collapsed on the bed in an uncontrollable fit of laughter. He laughed so much that the tears streamed from his eyes and his stomach hurt. He laughed so much that he rolled off the bed and tumbled to the hard floor.

Yes, for now at least, things really were back to normal.

The End

Also written by David Webb, published by:

Educational Printing Services Limited

The Library Ghost
ISBN 1-904374-66-2

Dinosaur Day
ISBN 1-904374-67-0

There's No Such Thing as an Alien
ISBN 1-900818-66-3

Laura's Game
ISBN 1-900818-61-2

Beneath the Bombers' Moon
ISBN 1-900818-33-7

Eye of the Storm
ISBN 1-900818-56-6

Sparky's Return
ISBN 1-900818-31-0

On Thin Ice
ISBN 1-900818-26-4

Educational Printing Services Limited publish a full range of teachers' resources, pupils' booklets and paperbacks.

For more information see our website.

Order on-line @ www.eprint.co.uk.